Jean Ingelow

A Story of Doom, and Other Poems

Jean Ingelow

A Story of Doom, and Other Poems

ISBN/EAN: 9783337388423

Printed in Europe, USA, Canada, Australia, Japan

Cover: Foto ©Andreas Hilbeck / pixelio.de

More available books at **www.hansebooks.com**

A

STORY OF DOOM

AND OTHER POEMS

BY

JEAN INGELOW

BOSTON
ROBERTS BROTHERS
1867

CONTENTS.

POEMS.

THE DREAMS THAT CAME TRUE.

 SAW in a vision once, our mother-sphere
    The world, her fixed foredoomèd oval tracing,
    Rolling and rolling on and resting never,
  While like a phantom fell, behind her pacing
The unfurled flag of night, her shadow drear
  Fled as she fled and hung to her forever.

Great Heaven! methought, how strange a doom to share.
  Would I may never bear
  Inevitable darkness after me
(Darkness endowed with drawings strong,
  And shadowy hands that cling unendingly),
  Nor feel that phantom-wings behind me sweep,
As she feels night pursuing through the long
  Illimitable reaches of " the vasty deep."

God save you, gentlefolks. There was a man
  Who lay awake at midnight on his bed,

Watching the spiral flame that feeding ran
   Among the logs upon his hearth, and shed
A comfortable glow, both warm and dim,
On crimson curtains that encompassed him.

Right stately was his chamber, soft and white
   The pillow, and his quilt was eider-down.
What mattered it to him though all that night
   The desolate driving cloud might lower and frown,
And winds were up the eddying sleet to chase,
That drave and drave and found no settling-place ?

What mattered it that leafless trees might rock,
   Or snow might drift athwart his window-pane ?
He bare a charméd life against their shock,
   Secure from cold, hunger, and weather stain ;
Fixed in his right, and born to good estate,
From common ills set by and separate.

From work and want and fear of want apart,
   This man (men called him Justice Wilvermore), —
This man had comforted his cheerful heart
   With all that it desired from every shore.
He had a right, — the right of gold is strong, —
He stood upon his right his whole life long.

Custom makes all things easy, and content
   Is careless, therefore on the storm and cold,
As he lay waking, never a thought he spent,

Albeit across the vale beneath the wold,
Along a reedy mere that frozen lay,
A range of sordid hovels stretched away.

What cause had he to think on them, forsooth ?
    What cause that night beyond another night ?
He was familiar even from his youth
    With their long ruin and their evil plight.
The wintry wind would search them like a scout,
The water froze within as freely as without.

He think upon them?   No!   They were forlorn,
    So were the cowering inmates whom they held ;
A thriftless tribe, to shifts and leanness born,
    Ever complaining : infancy or eld
Alike.   But there was rent, or long ago
Those cottage roofs had met with overthrow.

For this they stood ; and what his thoughts might be
    That winter night, I know not ; but I know
That, while the creeping flame fed silently
    And cast upon his bed a crimson glow,
The Justice slept, and shortly in his sleep
He fell to dreaming, and his dream was deep.

He dreamed that over him a shadow came ;
    And when he looked to find the cause, behold
Some person knelt between him and the flame : —
    A cowering figure of one frail and old, —

A woman; and she prayed as he descried,
And spread her feeble hands, and shook and sighed.

" Good Heaven ! " the Justice cried, and being dis-
          traught
    He called not to her, but he looked again :
She wore a tattered cloak, but she had naught
    Upon her head ; and she did quake amain,
And spread her wasted hands and poor attire
To gather in the brightness of his fire.

" I know you, woman ! " then the Justice cried ;
    " I know that woman well," he cried aloud ;
" The shepherd Aveland's widow : God me guide !
    A pauper kneeling on my hearth " : and bowed
The hag, like one at home, its warmth to share !
" How dares she to intrude ?   What does she here ?

" Ho, woman, ho ! " — but yet she did not stir,
    Though from her lips a fitful plaining broke ;
" I 'll ring my people up to deal with her ;
    I 'll rouse the house," he cried ; but while he spoke
He turned, and saw, but distant from his bed,
Another form, — a Darkness with a head.

Then in a rage, he shouted, " Who are you ? "
    For little in the gloom he might discern.
" Speak out ; speak now ; or I will make you rue
    The hour ! " but there was silence, and a stern,

Dark face from out the dusk appeared to lean,
And then again drew back, and was not seen.

"God!" cried the dreaming man, right impiously,
   "What have I done, that these my sleep affray?"
"God!" said the Phantom, "I appeal to Thee,
   Appoint Thou me this man to be my prey."
"God!" sighed the kneeling woman, frail and old,
"I pray Thee take me, for the world is cold."

Then said the trembling Justice, in affright,
   "Fiend, I adjure thee, speak thine errand here!"
And lo! it pointed in the failing light
   Toward the woman, answering, cold and clear,
"Thou art ordained an answer to thy prayer;
But first to tell *her* tale that kneeleth there."

"*Her* tale!" the Justice cried. "A pauper's tale!"
   And he took heart at this so low behest,
And let the stoutness of his will prevail,
   Demanding, "Is't for *her* you break my rest?
She went to jail of late for stealing wood,
She will again for this night's hardihood.

"I sent her; and to-morrow, as I live,
   I will commit her for this trespass here."
"Thou wilt not!" quoth the Shadow, "thou wilt give
   Her story words"; and then it stalked anear
And showed a lowering face, and, dread to see,
A countenance of angered majesty.

Then said the Justice, all his thoughts astray,
  With that material Darkness chiding him,
" If this must be, then speak to her, I pray,
  And bid her move, for all the room is dim
By reason of the place she holds to-night :
She kneels between me and the warmth and light."

" With adjurations deep and drawings strong,
  And with the power," it said, " unto me given,
I call upon thee, man, to tell thy wrong,
  Or look no more upon the face of Heaven.
Speak ! though she kneel throughout the livelong night,
And yet shall kneel between thee and the light."

This when the Justice heard, he raised his hands,
  And held them as the dead in effigy
Hold theirs, when carved upon a tomb.   The bands
  Of fate had bound him fast : no remedy
Was left : his voice unto himself was strange,
And that unearthly vision did not change.

He said, " That woman dwells anear my door,
  Her life and mine began the selfsame day,
And I am hale and hearty : from my store
  I never spared her aught : she takes her way
Of me unheeded ; pining, pinching care
Is all the portion that she has to share.

" She is a broken-down, poor, friendless wight,
  Through labor and through sorrow early old ;

And I have known of this her evil plight,
   Her scanty earnings, and her lodgment cold ;
A patienter poor soul shall ne'er be found :
She labored on my land the long year round.

" What wouldst thou have me say, thou fiend abhorred ?
   Show me no more thine awful visage grim.
If thou obey'st a greater, tell thy lord
   That I have paid her wages. Cry to him !
He has not *much* against me. None can say
I have not paid her wages day by day.

" The spell ! It draws me. I must speak again ;
   And speak against myself ; and speak aloud.
The woman once approached me to complain, —
   ' My wages are so low.' I may be proud ;
It is a fault." " Ay," quoth the Phantom fell,
" Sinner ! it is a fault : thou sayest well."

" She made her moan, ' My wages are so low.' "
   " Tell on !" " She said," he answered, " ' My best
     days
Are ended, and the summer is but slow
   To come ; and my good strength for work decays
By reason that I live so hard, and lie
On winter nights so bare for poverty.' "

" And you replied," — began the lowering shade,
   " And I replied," the Justice followed on,

" That wages like to mine my neighbor paid ;
   And if I raised the wages of the one
Straight should the others murmur ; furthermore,
The winter was as winters gone before.

" No colder and not longer."   " Afterward ? " —
   The Phantom questioned.   " Afterward," he groaned,
" She said my neighbor was a right good lord,
   Never a roof was broken that he owned ;
He gave much coal and clothing. ' Doth he so ?
Work for my neighbor, then,' I answered.   ' Go !

" ' You are full welcome.'   Then she mumbled out
   She hoped I was not angry ; hoped, forsooth,
I would forgive her : and I turned about,
   And said I should be angry in good truth
If this should be again, or ever more
She dared to stop me thus at the church door."

" Then ? " quoth the Shade ; and he, constrained, said on,
   " Then she, reproved, curtseyed herself away."
" Hast met her since ? " it made demand anon ;
   And after pause the Justice answered, " Ay ;
Some wood was stolen ; my people made a stir :
She was accused, and I did sentence her."

But yet, and yet, the dreaded questions came :
   " And didst thou weigh the matter, — taking thought
Upon her sober life and honest fame ? "

"I gave it," he replied, with gaze distraught;
"I gave it, Fiend, the usual care; I took
The usual pains; I could not nearer look,

"Because, — because their pilfering had got head.
  What wouldst thou more? The neighbors pleaded hard,
'T is true, and many tears the creature shed;
  But I had vowed their prayers to disregard,
Heavily strike the first that robbed my land,
And put down thieving with a steady hand.

"She said she was not guilty. Ay, 't is true
  She said so, but the poor are liars all.
O thou fell Fiend, what wilt thou? Must I view
  Thy darkness yet, and must thy shadow fall
Upon me miserable? I have done
No worse, no more than many a scathless one."

"Yet," quoth the Shade, "if ever to thine ears
  The knowledge of her blamelessness was brought,
Or others have confessed with dying tears
  The crime she suffered for, and thou hast wrought
All reparation in thy power, and told
Into her empty hand thy brightest gold: —

"If thou hast honored her, and hast proclaimed
  Her innocence and thy deploréd wrong,
Still thou art nought; for thou shalt yet be blamed
  In that she, feeble, came before thee strong,

1*

And thou, in cruel haste to deal a blow,
Because thou hadst been angered, worked her woe.

"But didst thou right her? Speak!" The Justice sighed,
  And beaded drops stood out upon his brow;
"How could I humble me," forlorn he cried,
  "To a base beggar? Nay, I will avow
That I did ill.   I will reveal the whole;
I kept that knowledge in my secret soul."

"Hear him!" the Phantom muttered; "hear this man,
  O changeless God upon the judgment throne."
With that, cold tremors through his pulses ran,
  And lamentably he did make his moan;
While, with its arms upraised above his head,
The dim dread visitor approached his bed.

"Into these doors," it said, "which thou hast closed,
  Daily this woman shall from henceforth come;
Her kneeling form shall yet be interposed
  Till all thy wretched hours have told their sum;
Shall yet be interposed by day, by night,
Between thee, sinner, and the warmth and light.

"Remembrance of her want shall make thy meal
  Like ashes, and thy wrong thou shalt not right.
But what!   Nay, verily, nor wealth nor weal
  From henceforth shall afford thy soul delight.
Till men shall lay thy head beneath the sod,
There shall be no deliverance, saith my God."

" Tell me thy name," the dreaming Justice cried ;
  " By what appointment dost thou doom me thus ? "
" 'T is well that thou shouldst know me," it replied,
  " For mine thou art, and nought shall sever us ;
From thine own lips and life I draw my force :
The name thy nation give me is REMORSE."

This when he heard, the dreaming man cried out,
  And woke affrighted ; and a crimson glow
The dying ember shed.   Within, without,
  In eddying rings the silence seemed to flow ;
The wind had lulled, and on his forehead shone
The last low gleam ; he was indeed alone.

" O, I have had a fearful dream," said he ;
  " I will take warning and for mercy trust ;
The fiend Remorse shall never dwell with me :
  I will repair that wrong, I will be just,
I will be kind, I will my ways amend."
Now the first dream is told unto its end.

Anigh the frozen mere a cottage stood,
  A piercing wind swept round and shook the door,
The shrunken door, and easy way made good,
  And drave long drifts of snow along the floor.
It sparkled there like diamonds, for the moon
Was shining in, and night was at the noon.

Before her dying embers, bent and pale,
  A woman sat because her bed was cold ;

She heard the wind, the driving sleet and hail,
  And she was hunger-bitten, weak and old;
Yet while she cowered, and while the casement shook,
Upon her trembling knees she held a book, —

A comfortable book for them that mourn,
  And good to raise the courage of the poor;
It lifts the veil and shows, beyond the bourne,
  Their Elder Brother, from His home secure,
That for them desolate He died to win,
Repeating, " Come, ye blessed, enter in."

What thought she on, this woman? on her days
  Of toil, or on the supperless night forlorn?
I think not so; the heart but seldom weighs
  With conscious care a burden always borne;
And she was used to these things, had grown old
In fellowship with toil, hunger, and cold.

Then did she think how sad it was to live
  Of all the good this world can yield bereft?
No, her untutored thoughts she did not give
  To such a theme; but in their warp and weft
She wove a prayer: then in the midnight deep
Faintly and slow she fell away to sleep.

A strange, a marvellous sleep, which brought a dream,
  And it was this: that all at once she heard
The pleasant babbling of a little stream

That ran beside her door, and then a bird
Broke out in songs. She looked, and lo! the rime
And snow had melted; it was summer time!

And all the cold was over, and the mere
   Full sweetly swayed the flags and rushes green;
The mellow sunlight poured right warm and clear
   Into her casement, and thereby were seen
Fair honeysuckle flowers, and wandering bees
Were hovering round the blossom-laden trees.

She said, "I will betake me to my door,
   And will look out and see this wondrous sight,
How summer is come back, and frost is o'er,
   And all the air warm waxen in a night."
With that she opened, but for fear she cried,
For lo! two Angels, — one on either side.

And while she looked, with marvelling measureless,
   The Angels stood conversing face to face,
But neither spoke to her. "The wilderness,"
   One Angel said, "the solitary place,
Shall yet be glad for Him." And then full fain
The other Angel answered, "He shall reign."

And when the woman heard, in wondering wise,
   She whispered, "They are speaking of my Lord."
And straightway swept across the open skies
   Multitudes like to these. They took the word,

That flock of Angels, " He shall come again,
My Lord, my Lord!" they sang, "and He shall reign!"

Then they, drawn up into the blue o'er-head,
   Right happy, shining ones, made haste to flee;
And those before her one to other said,
   " Behold He stands aneath yon almond-tree."
This when the woman heard, she fain had gazed,
But paused for reverence, and bowed down amazed.

After she looked, for this her dream was deep;
   She looked, and there was nought beneath the tree;
Yet did her love and longing overleap
   The fear of Angels, awful though they be,
And she passed out between the blessed things,
And brushed her mortal weeds against their wings.

O, all the happy world was in its best,
   The trees were covered thick with buds and flowers,
And these were dropping honey; for the rest,
   Sweetly the birds were piping in their bowers;
Across the grass did groups of Angels go,
And Saints in pairs were walking to and fro.

Then did she pass toward the almond-tree,
   And none she saw beneath it : yet each Saint
Upon his coming meekly bent the knee,
   And all their glory as they gazed waxed faint.
And then a 'lighting Angel neared the place,
And folded his fair wings before his face.

She also knelt, and spread her aged hands
  As feeling for the sacred human feet;
She said, " Mine eyes are held, but if He stands
  Anear, I will not let Him hence retreat
Except He bless me."   Then, O sweet ! O fair !
Some words were spoken, but she knew not where.

She knew not if beneath the boughs they woke,
  Or dropt upon her from the realms above ;
" What wilt thou, woman ? " in the dream He spoke,
  " Thy sorrow moveth Me, thyself I love ;
Long have I counted up thy mournful years,'
Once I did weep to wipe away thy tears."

She said : " My one Redeemer, only blest,
  I know Thy voice, and from my yearning heart
Draw out my deep desire, my great request,
  My prayer, that I might enter where Thou art.
Call me, O call from this world troublesome,
And let me see Thy face."   He answered, " Come."

Here is the ending of the second dream.
  It is a frosty morning, keen and cold,
Fast locked are silent mere and frozen stream,
  And snow lies sparkling on the desert wold ;
With savory morning meats they spread the board,
But Justice Wilvermore will walk abroad.

" Bring me my cloak," quoth he, as one in haste.
  " Before you breakfast, sir ? " his man replies.

"Ay," quoth he quickly, and he will not taste
   Of aught before him, but in urgent wise
As he would fain some carking care allay,
Across the frozen field he takes his way.

"A dream! how strange that it should move me so,
   'T was but a dream," quoth Justice Wilvermore:
"And yet I cannot peace nor pleasure know,
   For wrongs I have not heeded heretofore;
Silver and gear the crone shall have of me,
And dwell for life in yonder cottage free.

"For visions of the night are fearful things,
   Remorse is dread, though merely in a dream;
I will not subject me to visitings
   Of such a sort again. I will esteem
My peace above my pride. From natures rude
A little gold will buy me gratitude.

"The woman shall have leave to gather wood,
   As much as she may need, the long year round;
She shall, I say, — moreover, it were good
   Yon other cottage roofs to render sound.
Thus to my soul the ancient peace restore,
And sleep at ease," quoth Justice Wilvermore.

With that he nears the door: a frosty rime
   Is branching over it, and drifts are deep
Against the wall. He knocks, and there is time, —

(For none doth open), — time to list the sweep
And whistle of the wind along the mere
Through beds of stiffened reeds and rushes sere.

"If she be out, I have my pains for nought,"
   He saith, and knocks again, and yet once more,
But to his ear nor step nor stir is brought;
   And after pause, he doth unlatch the door
And enter. No: she is not out, for see
She sits asleep 'mid frost-work winterly.

Asleep, asleep before her empty grate,
   Asleep, asleep, albeit the landlord call.
"What, dame," he saith, and comes toward her
     straight,
   "Asleep so early!" But whate'er befall,
She sleepeth; then he nears her, and behold
He lays a hand on hers, and it is cold.

Then doth the Justice to his home return;
   From that day forth he wears a sadder brow;
His hands are opened, and his heart doth learn
   The patience of the poor. He made a vow
And keeps it, for the old and sick have shared
His gifts, their sordid homes he hath repaired.

And some he hath made happy, but for him
   Is happiness no more. He doth repent,
And now the light of joy is waxen dim,

B

Are all his steps toward the Highest sent;
He looks for mercy, and he waits release
Above, for this world doth not yield him peace.

Night after night, night after desolate night,
   Day after day, day after tedious day,
Stands by his fire, and dulls its gleamy light,
   Paceth behind or meets him in the way;
Or shares the path by hedgerow, mere, or stream,
The visitor that doomed him in his dream.

   Thy kingdom come.
I heard a Seer cry, — " The wilderness,
   The solitary place,
Shall yet be glad for Him, and He shall bless
(Thy kingdom come) with his revealéd face
The forests ; they shall drop their precious gum,
And shed for Him their balm : and He shall yield
The grandeur of His speech to charm the field.

" Then all the soothéd winds shall drop to listen,
   (Thy kingdom come,)
Comforted waters waxen calm shall glisten
With bashful tremblement beneath His smile :
   And Echo ever the while
Shall take, and in her awful joy repeat,
The laughter of His lips — (thy kingdom come) :
And hills that sit apart shall be no longer dumb ;

No, they shall shout and shout,
Raining their lovely loyalty along the dewy plain :
And valleys round about,

" And all the well-contented land, made sweet
With flowers she opened at His feet,
Shall answer ; shout and make the welkin ring
And tell it to the stars, shout, shout, and sing ;
Her cup being full to the brim,
Her poverty made rich with Him,
Her yearning satisfied to its utmost sum, —
Lift up thy voice, O earth, prepare thy song,
It shall not yet be long,
Lift up, O earth, for He shall come again,
Thy Lord ; and He shall reign, and He SHALL reign, —
Thy kingdom come."

SONGS

ON

THE VOICES OF BIRDS.

SONGS ON THE VOICES OF BIRDS.

INTRODUCTION.

CHILD AND BOATMAN.

"MARTIN, I wonder who makes all the songs."
  "You do, sir?"
                "Yes, I wonder how they come."
"Well, boy, I wonder what you'll wonder next!"
"But somebody must make them?"
                                "Sure enough."
"Does your wife know?"
                "She never said she did."
"You told me that she knew so many things."
"I said she was a London woman, sir,
And a fine scholar, but I never said
She knew about the songs."
                "I wish she did."
"And I wish no such thing; she knows enough,
She knows too much already. Look you now,
This vessel's off the stocks, a tidy craft."
"A schooner, Martin?"
                "No, boy, no; a brig,
Only she's schooner rigged,—a lovely craft."

"Is she for me?   O, thank you, Martin, dear.
What shall I call her?"

"Well, sir, what you please."
"Then write on her 'The Eagle.'"

"Bless the child!
Eagle! why, you know naught of eagles, you.
When we lay off the coast, up Canada way,
And chanced to be ashore when twilight fell,
That was the place for eagles; bald they were,
With eyes as yellow as gold."

"O, Martin, dear,
Tell me about them."

"Tell! there's nought to tell,
Only they snored o' nights and frighted us."
"Snored?"

"Ay, I tell you, snored; they slept upright
In the great oaks by scores; as true as time,
If I'd had aught upon my mind just then,
I would n't have walked that wood for unknown gold;
It was most awful.   When the moon was full,
I've seen them fish at night, in the middle watch,
When she got low.   I've seen them plunge like stones,
And come up fighting with a fish as long,
Ay, longer than my arm; and they would sail,—
When they had struck its life out,— they would sail
Over the deck, and show their fell, fierce eyes,
And croon for pleasure, hug the prey, and speed
Grand as a frigate on a wind."

"My ship,

She must be called 'The Eagle' after these.
And, Martin, ask your wife about the songs
When you go in at dinner-time."

"Not I."

THE NIGHTINGALE HEARD BY THE UNSATISFIED HEART

WHEN in a May-day hush
    Chanteth the Missel-thrush
The harp o' the heart makes answer with murmurous
        stirs ;
    When Robin-redbreast sings,
    We think on budding springs,
And Culvers when they coo are love's remembrancers.

    But thou in the trance of light
    Stayest the feeding night,
And Echo makes sweet her lips with the utterance wise,
    And casts at our glad feet,
    In a wisp of fancies fleet,
Life's fair, life's unfulfilled, impassioned prophecies.

    Her central thought full well
    Thou hast the wit to tell,
To take the sense o' the dark and to yield it so ;

2

The moral of moonlight
To set in a cadence bright,
And sing our loftiest dream that we thought none did
know.

I have no nest as thou,
Bird on the blossoming bough,
Yet over thy tongue outfloweth the song o' my soul,
Chanting, " forego thy strife,
The spirit out-acts the life,
But MUCH is seldom theirs who can perceive THE WHOLE.

" Thou drawest a perfect lot
All thine, but holden not,
Lie low, at the feet of beauty that ever shall bide ;
There might be sorer smart
Than thine, far-seeing heart,
Whose fate is still to yearn, and not be satisfied."

SAND MARTINS.

I PASSED an inland-cliff precipitate ;
From tiny caves peeped many a sooty poll ;
In each a mother-martin sat elate,
And of the news delivered her small soul.

Fantastic chatter! hasty, glad, and gay,
   Whereof the meaning was not ill to tell:
"Gossip, how wags the world with you to-day?"
   "Gossip, the world wags well, the world wags well."

And heark'ning, I was sure their little ones
   Were in the bird-talk, and discourse was made
Concerning hot sea-bights and tropic suns,
   For a clear sultriness the tune conveyed;—

And visions of the sky as of a cup
   Hailing down light on pagan Pharaoh's sand,
And quivering air-waves trembling up and up,
   And blank stone faces marvellously bland.

"When should the young be fledged and with them hie
   Where costly day drops down in crimson light?
(Fortunate countries of the firefly
   Swarm with blue diamonds all the sultry night,

"And the immortal moon takes turn with them.)
   When should they pass again by that red land,
Where lovely mirage works a broidered hem
   To fringe with phantom-palms a robe of sand?

"When should they dip their breasts again and play
   In slumberous azure pools, clear as the air,
Where rosy-winged flamingoes fish all day,
   Stalking amid the lotus blossom fair?

" Then, over podded tamarinds bear their flight,
   While cassias blossom in the zone of calms,
And so betake them to a south sea-bight,
   To gossip in the crowns of cocoa-palms

" Whose roots are in the spray.   O, haply there
   Some dawn, white-wingéd they might chance to find
A frigate standing in to make more fair
   The loneliness unaltered of mankind.

" A frigate come to water: nuts would fall,
   And nimble feet would climb the flower-flushed
      strand,
While northern talk would ring, and there withal
   The martins would desire the cool north land.

" And all would be as it had been before ;
   Again at eve there would be news to tell ;
Who passed should hear them chant it o'er and o'er,
   ' Gossip, how wags the world ?'   ' Well, gossip,
      well.' "

A POET IN HIS YOUTH, AND THE CUCKOO-BIRD.

ONCE upon a time, I lay
   Fast asleep at dawn of day;
Windows open to the south,
Fancy pouting her sweet mouth
To my ear.
          She turned a globe
In her slender hand, her robe
Was all spangled; and she said,
As she sat at my bed's head,
"Poet, poet, what, asleep!
Look! the ray runs up the steep
To your roof." Then in the golden
Essence of romances olden,
Bathed she my entrancèd heart.
And she gave a hand to me,
Drew me onward, "Come!" said she;
And she moved with me apart,
Down the lovely vale of Leisure.

Such its name was, I heard say,
For some Fairies trooped that way;
Common people of the place,
Taking their accustomed pleasure,
(All the clocks being stopped) to race

Down the slope on palfreys fleet.
Bridle bells made tinkling sweet;
And they said, "What signified
Faring home till eventide:
There were pies on every shelf,
And the bread would bake itself."
But for that I cared not, fed,
As it were, with angels' bread,
Sweet as honey; yet next day
All foredoomed to melt away;
Gone before the sun waxed hot,
Melted manna that *was not*.

Rock-doves' poetry of plaint,
Or the starling's courtship quaint;
Heart made much of, 't was a boon
Won from silence, and too soon
Wasted in the ample air:
Building rooks far distant were.
Scarce at all would speak the rills,
And I saw the idle hills,
In their amber hazes deep,
Fold themselves and go to sleep,
Though it was not yet high noon.

Silence?   Rather music brought
From the spheres !   As if a thought,
Having taken wings, did fly
Through the reaches of the sky.

Silence? No, a sumptuous sigh
That had found embodiment,
That had come across the deep
After months of wintry sleep,
And with tender heavings went
Floating up the firmament.

" O," I mourned, half slumbering yet,
" 'T is the voice of *my* regret, —
Mine! " and I awoke. Full sweet
Saffron sunbeams did me greet;
And the voice it spake again,
Dropped from yon blue cup of light
Or some cloudlet swan's-down white
On my soul, that drank full fain
The sharp joy — the sweet pain —
Of its clear, right innocent,
Unreprovéd discontent.

How it came — where it went —
Who can tell? The open blue
Quivered with it, and I, too,
Trembled. I remembered me
Of the springs that used to be,
When a dimpled white-haired child,
Shy and tender and half wild,
In the meadows I had heard
Some way off the talking bird,
And had felt it marvellous sweet,

For it laughed: it did me greet,
Calling me: yet, hid away
In the woods, it would not play.
No.

And all the world about,
While a man will work or sing,
Or a child pluck flowers of spring,
Thou wilt scatter music out,
Rouse him with thy wandering note,
Changeful fancies set afloat,
Almost tell with thy clear throat,
But not quite, — the wonder-rife,
Most sweet riddle, dark and dim,
That he searcheth all his life,
Searcheth yet, and ne'er expoundeth;
And so winnowing of thy wings,
Touch and trouble his heart's strings,
That a certain music soundeth
In that wondrous instrument,
With a trembling upward sent,
That is reckoned sweet above
By the Greatness surnamed Love.

" O, I hear thee in the blue;
Would that I might wing it too!
O to have what hope hath seen!
O to be what might have been!

" O to set my life, sweet bird,
To a tune that oft I heard
When I used to stand alone
Listening to the lovely moan
Of the swaying pines o'erhead,
While, a-gathering of bee-bread
For their living, murmured round,
As the pollen dropped to ground,
All the nations from the hives ;
And the little brooding wives
On each nest, brown dusky things,
Sat with gold-dust on their wings.
Then beyond (more sweet than all)
Talked the tumbling waterfall ;
And there were, and there were not
(As might fall, and form anew
Bell-hung drops of honey-dew)
Echoes of — I know not what ;
As if some right-joyous elf,
While about his own affairs,
Whistled softly otherwheres.
Nay, as if our mother dear,
Wrapped in sun-warm atmosphere,
Laughed a little to herself,
Laughed a little as she rolled,
Thinking on the days of old.

" Ah ! there be some hearts, I wis,
To which nothing comes amiss.

Mine was one.   Much secret wealth
I was heir to : and by stealth,
When the moon was fully grown,
And she thought herself alone,
I have heard her, ay, right well,
Shoot a silver message down
To the unseen sentinel
Of a still, snow-thatchéd town.

" Once, awhile ago, I peered
In the nest where Spring was reared.
There, she quivering her fair wings,
Flattered March with chirrupings ;
And they fed her ; nights and days,
Fed her mouth with much sweet food,
And her heart with love and praise,
Till the wild thing rose and flew
Over woods and water-springs,
Shaking off the morning dew
In a rainbow from her wings.

" Once (I will to you confide
More), O once in forest wide,
I, benighted, overheard
Marvellous mild echoes stirred,
And a calling half defined,
And an answering from afar ;
Somewhat talkéd with a star,
And the talk was of mankind.

"' Cuckoo, cuckoo!'
Float anear in upper blue:
Art thou yet a prophet true?
Wilt thou say, 'And having seen
Things that be, and have not been,
Thou art free o' the world, for naught
Can despoil thee of thy thought'?
Nay, but make me music yet,
Bird, as deep as my regret,
For a certain hope hath set,
Like a star; and left me heir
To a crying for its light,
An aspiring infinite,
And a beautiful despair!

"Ah! no more, no more, no more
I shall lie at thy shut door,
Mine ideal, my desired,
Dreaming thou wilt open it,
And step out, thou most admired,
By my side to fare, or sit,
Quenching hunger and all drouth
With the wit of thy fair mouth,
Showing me the wishéd prize
In the calm of thy dove's eyes,
Teaching me the wonder-rife
Majesties of human life,
All its fairest possible sum,
And the grace of its to come.

" What a difference ! Why of late
All sweet music used to say,
' She will come, and with thee stay
To-morrow, man, if not to-day.'
Now it murmurs, ' Wait, wait, wait !' "

A RAVEN IN A WHITE CHINE.

I SAW when I looked up, on either hand,
   A pale high chalk-cliff, reared aloft in white ;
A narrowing rent soon closed toward the land, —
   Toward the sea, an open yawning bight.

The polished tide, with scarce a hint of blue,
   Washed in the bight ; above with angry moan
A raven, that was robbed, sat up in view,
   Croaking and crying on a ledge alone.

" Stand on thy nest, spread out thy fateful wings,
   With sullen hungry love bemoan thy brood,
For boys have wrung their necks, those imp-like things,
   Whose beaks dripped crimson daily at their food.

" Cry, thou black prophetess ! cry, and despair,
   None love thee, none ! Their father was thy foe,
Whose father in his youth did know thy lair,
   And steal thy little demons long ago.

" Thou madest many childless for their sake,
    And picked out many eyes that loved the light.
Cry, thou black prophetess ! sit up, awake,
    Forebode; and ban them through the desolate night."

Lo ! while I spake it, with a crimson hue
    The dipping sun endowed that silver flood,
And all the cliffs flushed red, and up she flew,
    The bird, as mad to bathe in airy blood.

" Nay, thou mayst cry, the omen is not thine,
    Thou aged priestess of fell doom, and fate.
It is not blood : thy gods are making wine,
    They spilt the must outside their city gate,

" And stained their azure pavement with the lees :
    They will not listen though thou cry aloud.
Old Chance, thy dame, sits mumbling at her ease,
    Nor hears ; the fair hag, Luck, is in her shroud.

" They heed not, they withdraw the sky-hung sign :
    Thou hast no charm against the favorite race ;
Thy gods pour out for it, not blood, but wine :
    There is no justice in their dwelling-place !

" Safe in their father's house the boys shall rest,
    Though thy fell brood doth stark and silent lie ;
Their unborn sons may yet despoil thy nest :
    Cry, thou black prophetess ! lift up ! cry, cry !"

THE WARBLING OF BLACKBIRDS.

WHEN I hear the waters fretting,
    When I see the chestnut letting
All her lovely blossom falter down, I think, "Alas the
        day!"
    Once with magical sweet singing,
    Blackbirds set the woodland ringing,
That awakes no more while April hours wear themselves
        away.

    In our hearts fair hope lay smiling,
    Sweet as air, and all beguiling;
And there hung a mist of bluebells on the slope and down
        the dell;
    And we talked of joy and splendor
    That the years unborn would render,
And the blackbirds helped us with the story, for they knew
        it well.

    Piping, fluting, " Bees are humming,
    April 's here, and summer 's coming;
Don't forget us when you walk, a man with men, in pride
        and joy;
    Think on us in alleys shady,
    When you step a graceful lady;
For no fairer day have we to hope for, little girl and boy.

" Laugh and play, O lisping waters,
Lull our downy sons and daughters ;
Come, O wind, and rock their leafy cradle in thy wander-
          ings coy ;
When they wake we 'll end the measure
With a wild sweet cry of pleasure,
And a ' Hey down derry, let 's be merry ! little girl and
          boy !' "

SEA-MEWS IN WINTER TIME.

I WALKED beside a dark gray sea,
    And said, " O world, how cold thou art !
Thou poor white world, I pity thee,
    For joy and warmth from thee depart.

" Yon rising wave licks off the snow,
    Winds on the crag each other chase,
In little powdery whirls they blow
    The misty fragments down its face.

" The sea is cold, and dark its rim,
    Winter sits cowering on the wold,
And I beside this watery brim,
    Am also lonely, also cold."

I spoke, and drew toward a rock,
　　Where many mews made twittering sweet;
Their wings upreared, the clustering flock
　　Did pat the sea-grass with their feet.

A rock but half submerged, the sea
　　Ran up and washed it while they fed;
Their fond and foolish ecstasy
　　A wondering in my fancy bred.

Joy companied with every cry,
　　Joy in their food, in that keen wind,
That heaving sea, that shaded sky,
　　And in themselves, and in their kind.

The phantoms of the deep at play!
　　What idless graced the twittering things;
Luxurious paddlings in the spray,
　　And delicate lifting up of wings.

Then all at once a flight, and fast
　　The lovely crowd flew out to sea;
If mine own life had been recast,
　　Earth had not looked more changed to me.

" Where is the cold?　Yon clouded skies
　　Have only dropt their curtains low
To shade the old mother where she lies
　　Sleeping a little, 'neath the snow.

" The cold is not in crag, nor scar,
   Not in the snows that lap the lea,
Not in yon wings that beat afar,
   Delighting, on the crested sea ;

" No, nor in yon exultant wind
   That shakes the oak and bends the pine.
Look near, look in, and thou shalt find
   No sense of cold, fond fool, but thine ! "

With that I felt the gloom depart,
   And thoughts within me did unfold,
Whose sunshine warmed me to the heart, —
   I walked in joy, and was not cold.

LAURANCE.

E knew she did not love him; but so long
As rivals were unknown to him, he dwelt
At ease, and did not find his love a pain.

He had much deference in his nature, need
To honor — it became him; he was frank,
Fresh, hardy, of a joyous mind, and strong, —
Looked all things straight in the face. So when she came
Before him first, he looked at her, and looked
No more, but colored to his healthful brow,
And wished himself a better man, and thought
On certain things, and wished they were undone,
Because her girlish innocence, the grace
Of her umblemished pureness, wrought in him
A longing and aspiring, and a shame
To think how wicked was the world, — that world
Which he must walk in, — while from her (and such
As she was) it was hidden; there was made
A clean path, and the girl moved on like one
In some enchanted ring.

In his young heart
She reigned, with all the beauties that she had,
And all the virtues that he rightly took
For granted; there he set her with her crown,
And at her first enthronement he turned out
Much that was best away, for unaware
His thoughts grew noble.   She was always there
And knew it not, and he grew like to her
And like to what he thought her.

                 Now he dwelt
With kin that loved him well, — two fine old folk,
A rich, right honest yeoman, and his dame, —
Their only grandson he, their pride, their heir.

To these, one daughter had been born, one child,
And as she grew to woman, "Look," they said,
"She must not leave us; let us build a wing,
With cheerful rooms and wide, to our old grange;
There may she dwell, with her good man, and all
God sends them."   Then the girl in her first youth
Married a curate, — handsome, poor in purse,
Of gentle blood and manners, and he lived
Under her father's roof, as they had planned.

Full soon, for happy years are short, they filled
The house with children; four were born to them.
Then came a sickly season; fever spread
   Among the poor.   The curate, never slack
   In duty, praying by the sick, or worse,

Burying the dead, when all the air was clogged
With poisonous mist, was stricken ; long he lay
Sick, almost to the death, and when his head
He lifted from the pillow, there was left
One only of that pretty flock : his girls,
His three, were cold beneath the sod ; his boy,
Their eldest born, remained.

            The drooping wife
Bore her great sorrow in such quiet wise,
That first they marvelled at her, then they tried
To rouse her, showing her their bitter grief,
Lamenting, and not sparing ; but she sighed,
" Let me alone, it will not be for long."
Then did her mother tremble, murmuring out,
" Dear child, the best of comfort will be soon.
O, when you see this other little face,
You will, please God, be comforted."

                 She said,
" I shall not live to see it " ; but she did, —
A little sickly face, a wan, thin face.
Then she grew eager, and her eyes were bright
When she would plead with them : " Take me away,
Let me go south ; it is the bitter blast
That chills my tender babe ; she cannot thrive
Under the desolate, dull, mournful cloud."
Then all they journeyed south together, mute
With past and coming sorrow, till the sun,
In gardens edging the blue tideless main,
Warmed them and calmed the aching at their hearts,

And all went better for a while; but not
For long.   They sitting by the orange-trees
Once rested, and the wife was very still:
One woman with narcissus flowers heaped up
Let down her basket from her head, but paused
With pitying gesture, and drew near and stooped,
Taking a white wild face upon her breast, —
The little babe on its poor mother's knees,
None marking it, none knowing else, had died.

The fading mother could not stay behind,
Her heart was broken; but it awed them most
To feel they must not, dared not, pray for life,
Seeing she longed to go, and went so gladly.

After, these three, who loved each other well,
Brought their one child away, and they were best
Together in the wide old grange.   Full oft
The father with the mother talked of her,
Their daughter, but the husband nevermore;
He looked for solace in his work, and gave
His mind to teach his boy.   And time went on,
Until the grandsire prayed those other two
" Now part with him; it must be; for his good:
He rules and knows it; choose for him a school,
Let him have all advantages, and all
Good training that should make a gentleman."

With that they parted from their boy, and lived

Longing between his holidays, and time
Sped; he grew on till he had eighteen years.
His father loved him, wished to make of him
Another parson; but the farmer's wife
Murmured at that: " No, no, they learned bad ways,
They ran in debt at college; she had heard
That many rued the day they sent their boys
To college "; and between the two broke in
His grandsire: " Find a sober, honest man,
A scholar, for our lad should see the world
While he is young, that he may marry young.
He will not settle and be satisfied
Till he has run about the world awhile.
Good lack, I longed to travel in my youth,
And had no chance to do it.   Send him off,
A sober man being found to trust him with,
One with the fear of God before his eyes."
And he prevailed; the careful father chose
A tutor, young, — the worthy matron thought, —
In truth, not ten years older than her boy,
And glad as he to range, and keen for snows,
Desert, and ocean.   And they made strange choice
Of where to go, left the sweet day behind,
And pushed up north in whaling ships, to feel
What cold was, see the blowing whale come up,
And Arctic creatures, while a scarlet sun
Went round and round, crowd on the clear blue berg.

Then did the trappers have them; and they heard

Nightly the whistling calls of forest-men
That mocked the forest wonners; and they saw
Over the open, raging up like doom,
The dangerous dust-cloud, that was full of eyes, —
The bisons. So were three years gone like one;
And the old cities drew them for a while,
Great mothers, by the Tiber and the Seine;
They have hid many sons hard by their seats,
But all the air is stirring with them still,
The waters murmur of them, skies at eve
Are stained with their rich blood, and every sound
Means men.

        At last, the fourth year running out,
The youth came home. And all the cheerful house
Was decked in fresher colors, and the dame
Was full of joy. But in the father's heart
Abode a painful doubt. "It is not well;
He cannot spend his life with dog and gun.
I do not care that my one son should sleep
Merely for keeping him in breath, and wake
Only to ride to cover."

            Not the less
The grandsire pondered. "Ay, the boy must WORK
Or SPEND; and I must let him spend; just stay
Awhile with us, and then from time to time
Have leave to be away with those fine folk
With whom, these many years, at school, and now,
During his sojourn in the foreign towns,
He has been made familiar." Thus a month

Went by. They liked the stirring ways of youth,
The quick elastic step, and joyous mind,
Ever expectant of it knew not what,
But something higher than has e'er been born
Of easy slumber and sweet competence.
And as for him, — the while they thought and thought
A comfortable instinct let him know
How they had waited for him, to complete
And give a meaning to their lives ; and still
At home, but with a sense of newness there,
And frank and fresh as in the school-boy days,
He oft — invading of his father's haunts,
The study where he passed the silent morn —
Would sit, devouring with a greedy joy
The piled-up books, uncut as yet ; or wake
To guide with him by night the tube, and search,
Ay, think to find new stars ; then risen betimes,
Would ride about the farm, and list the talk
Of his hale grandsire.

                    But a day came round,
When, after peering in his mother's room,
Shaded and shuttered from the light, he oped
A door, and found the rosy grandmother
Ensconced and happy in her special pride,
Her storeroom.   She was corking syrups rare,
And fruits all sparkling in a crystal coat.
Here after choice of certain cates well known,
He, sitting on her bacon-chest at ease,
Sang as he watched her, till right suddenly,

As if a new thought came, " Goody," quoth he,
" What, think you, do they want to do with me?
What have they planned for me that I should do?"

" Do, laddie!" quoth she faltering, half in tears;
" Are you not happy with us, not content?
Why would ye go away?   There is no need
That ye should DO at all.   O, bide at home.
Have we not plenty?"
                    " Even so," he said;
" I did not wish to go."
                    ". Nay, then," quoth she,
" Be idle; let me see your blessed face.
What, is the horse your father chose for you
Not to your mind?   He is?   Well, well, remain;
Do as you will, so you but do it here.
You shall not want for money."
                              But, his arms
Folding, he sat and twisted up his mouth
With comical discomfiture.
                          " What, then,"
She sighed, " what is it, child, that you would like?"
" Why," said he, " farming."
                          And she looked at him,
Fond, foolish woman that she was, to find
Some fitness in the worker for the work,
And she found none.   A certain grace there was
Of movement, and a beauty in the face,
Sun-browned and healthful beauty that had come

From his grave father; and she thought, "Good lack,
A farmer! he is fitter for a duke.
He walks; why, how he walks! if I should meet
One like him, whom I knew not, I should ask,
And who may that be?" So the foolish thought
Found words. Quoth she, half laughing, half ashamed,
"We planned to make of you — a gentleman."
And with engaging sweet audacity
She thought it nothing less, — he, looking up,
With a smile in his blue eyes, replied to her,
"And hav'n't you done it?" Quoth she, lovingly,
"I think we have, laddie; I think we have."

"Then," quoth he, "I may do what best I like;
It makes no matter. Goody, you were wise
To help me in it, and to let me farm;
I think of getting into mischief else!"
"No! do ye, laddie?" quoth the dame, and laughed.
"But ask my grandfather," the youth went on,
"To let me have the farm he bought last year,
The little one, to manage. I like land;
I want some." And she, womanlike, gave way
Convinced; and promised, and made good her word,
And that same night upon the matter spoke,
In presence of the father and the son.

"Roger," quoth she, "our Laurance wants to farm;
I think he might do worse." The father sat
Mute but right glad. The grandson breaking in

Set all his wish and his ambition forth;
But cunningly the old man hid his joy,
And made conditions with a faint demur.
Then pausing, " Let your father speak," quoth he ;
" I am content if he is ": at his word
The parson took him, ay, and, parson like,
Put a religious meaning in the work,
Man's earliest work, and wished his son God speed.

II.

Thus all were satisfied, and day by day,
For two sweet years a happy course was theirs ;
Happy, but yet the fortunate, the young
Loved, and much cared-for, entered on his strife, —
A stirring of the heart, a quickening keen
Of sight and hearing to the delicate
Beauty and music of an altered world;
Began to walk in that mysterious light
Which doth reveal and yet transform ; which gives
Destiny, sorrow, youth, and death, and life,
Intenser meaning; in disquieting
Lifts up ; a shining light : men call it Love.

Fair, modest eyes had she, the girl he loved ;
A silent creature, thoughtful, grave, sincere.
She never turned from him with sweet caprice,
Nor changing moved his soul to troublous hope,
Nor dropped for him her heavy lashes low,

But excellent in youthful grace came up;
And ere his words were ready, passing on,
Had left him all a-tremble; yet made sure
That by her own true will, and fixed intent,
She held him thus remote.   Therefore, albeit
He knew she did not love him, yet so long
As of a rival unaware, he dwelt
All in the present, without fear, or hope,
Enthralled and whelmed in the deep sea of love,
And could not get his head above its wave
To reach the far horizon, or to mark
Whereto it drifted him.

     So long, so long;
Then, on a sudden, came the ruthless fate,
Showed him a bitter truth, and brought him bale
All in the tolling out of noon.

       'T was thus:
Snow-time was come; it had been snowing hard;
Across the churchyard path he walked; the clock
Began to strike, and, as he passed the porch,
Half turning, through a sense that came to him
As of some presence in it, he beheld
His love, and she had come for shelter there;
And all her face was fair with rosy bloom,
The blush of happiness; and one held up
Her ungloved hand in both his own, and stooped
Toward it, sitting by her.   O her eyes
Were full of peace and tender light: they looked
One moment in the ungraced lover's face

While he was passing in the snow; and he
Received the story, while he raised his hat
Retiring.   Then the clock left off to strike,
And that was all.   It snowed, and he walked on;
And in a certain way he marked the snow,
And walked, and came upon the open heath;
And in a certain way he marked the cold,
And walked as one that had no starting-place
Might walk, but not to any certain goal.

And he strode on toward a hollow part,
Where from the hillside gravel had been dug,
And he was conscious of a cry, and went
Dulled in his sense, as though he heard it not;
Till a small farmhouse drudge, a half-grown girl,
Rose from the shelter of a drift that lay
Against the bushes, crying, " God ! O God,
O my good God, He sends us help at last."

Then looking hard upon her, came to him
The power to feel and to perceive.   Her teeth
Chattered, and all her limbs with shuddering failed,
And in her threadbare shawl was wrapped a child
That looked on him with wondering, wistful eyes.

" I thought to freeze," the girl broke out with tears;
" Kind sir, kind sir," and she held out the child,
As praying him to take it ; and he did;
And gave to her the shawl, and swathed his charge

In the foldings of his plaid; and when it thrust
Its small round face against his breast, and felt
With small red hands for warmth, — unbearable
Pains of great pity rent his straitened heart,
For the poor upland dwellers had been out
Since morning dawn, at early milking-time,
Wandering and stumbling in the drift.   And now,
Lamed with a fall, half crippled by the cold,
Hardly prevailed his arm to drag her on,
That ill-clad child, who yet the younger child
Had motherly cared to shield.   So toiling through
The great white storm coming, and coming yet,
And coming till the world confounded sat
With all her fair familiar features gone,
The mountains muffled in an eddying swirl,
He led or bore them, and the little one
Peered from her shelter, pleased; but oft would mourn
The elder, " They will beat me: O my can,
I left my can of milk upon the moor.
And he compared her trouble with his own,
And had no heart to speak.   And yet 't was keen;
It filled her to the putting down of pain
And hunger, — what could his do more?

                                        He brought
The children to their home, and suddenly
Regained himself, and wondering at himself,
That he had borne, and yet been dumb so long,
The weary wailing of the girl: he paid
Money to buy her pardon; heard them say,

" Peace, we have feared for you ; forget the milk,
It is no matter!" and went forth again
And waded in the snow, and quietly
Considered in his patience what to do
With all the dull remainder of his days.

With dusk he was at home, and felt it good
To hear his kindred talking, for it broke
A mocking, endless echo in his soul,
" It is no matter!" and he could not choose
But mutter, though the weariness o'ercame
His spirit, " Peace, it is no matter ; peace,
It is no matter!"   For he felt that all
Was as it had been, and his father's heart
Was easy, knowing not how that same day
Hope with her tender colors and delight
(He should not care to have him know) were dead ;
Yea, to all these, his nearest and most dear,
It was no matter.   And he heard them talk
Of timber felled, of certain fruitful fields,
And profitable markets.
                                All for him
Their plans, and yet the echoes swarmed and swam
About his head, whenever there was pause ;
" It is no matter!"   And his greater self
Arose in him and fought.   " It matters much,
It matters all to these, that not to-day
Nor ever they should know it.   I will hide
The wound ; ay, hide it with a sleepless care.

What! shall I make these three to drink of rue,
Because my cup is bitter?" And he thrust
Himself in thought away, and made his ears
Hearken, and caused his voice, that yet did seem
Another, to make answer, when they spoke,
As there had been no snowstorm, and no porch,
And no despair.

        So this went on awhile.
Until the snow had melted from the wold,
And he, one noonday, wandering up a lane,
Met on a turn the woman whom he loved.
Then, even to trembling he was moved: his speech
Faltered; but when the common kindly words
Of greeting were all said, and she passed on,
He could not bear her sweetness and his pain.
"Muriel!" he cried; and when she heard her name,
She turned. "You know I love you," he broke out:
She answered "Yes," and sighed.

        "O pardon me,
Pardon me," quoth the lover; "let me rest
In certainty, and hear it from your mouth:
Is he with whom I saw you once of late
To call you wife?" "I hope so," she replied;
And over all her face the rose-bloom came,
As thinking on that other, unaware
Her eyes waxed tender. When he looked on her,
Standing to answer him, with lovely shame,
Submiss, and yet not his, a passionate,
A quickened sense of his great impotence

To drive away the doom got hold on him;
He set his teeth to force the unbearable
Misery back, his wide-awakened eyes
Flashed as with flame.

        And she, all overawed
And mastered by his manhood, waited yet,
And trembled at the deep she could not sound;
A passionate nature in a storm; a heart
Wild with a mortal pain, and in the grasp
Of an immortal love.

        " Farewell," he said,
Recovering words, and when she gave her hand,
" My thanks for your good candor; for I feel
That it has cost you something." Then, the blush
Yet on her face, she said: " It was your due:
But keep this matter from your friends and kin,
We would not have it known." Then cold and proud,
Because there leaped from under his straight lids,
And instantly was veiled, a keen surprise, —
" He wills it, and I therefore think it well."
Thereon they parted; but from that time forth,
Whether they met on festal eve, in field,
Or at the church, she ever bore herself
Proudly, for she had felt a certain pain,
The disapproval hastily betrayed
And quickly hidden hurt her. " 'T was a grace,"
She thought, " to tell this man the thing he asked,
And he rewards me with surprise. I like
No one's surprise, and least of all bestowed

3*

Where he bestowed it."

     But the spring came on :
Looking to wed in April all her thoughts
Grew loving ; she would fain the world had waxed
More happy with her happiness, and oft
Walking among the flowery woods she felt
Their loveliness reach down into her heart,
And knew with them the ecstasies of growth,
The rapture that was satisfied with light,
The pleasure of the leaf in exquisite
Expansion, through the lovely longed-for spring.

And as for him, — (Some narrow hearts there are
That suffer blight when that they fed upon
As something to complete their being fails,
And they retire into their holds and pine,
And long restrained grow stern.   But some there are
That in a sacred want and hunger rise,
And draw the misery home and live with it,
And excellent in honor wait, and will
That somewhat good should yet be found in it,
Else wherefore were they born ?), — and as for him,
He loved her, but his peace and welfare made
The sunshine of three lives.   The cheerful grange
Threw open wide its hospitable doors
And drew in guests for him.   The garden flowers,
Sweet budding wonders, all were set for him.
In him the eyes at home were satisfied,
And if he did but laugh the ear approved.

What then ?   He dwelt among them as of old,
And taught his mouth to smile.

              And time went on,
Till on a morning, when the perfect spring
Rested among her leaves, he journeying home
After short sojourn in a neighboring town,
Stopped at the little station on the line
That ran between his woods ; a lonely place
And quiet, and a woman and a child
Got out.   He noted them, but walking on
Quickly, went back into the wood, impelled
By hope, for, passing, he had seen his love,
And she was sitting on a rustic seat
That overlooked the line, and he desired
With longing indescribable to look
Upon her face again.   And he drew near.
She was right happy ; she was waiting there.
He felt that she was waiting for her lord.
She cared no whit if Laurance went or stayed,
But answered when he spoke, and dropped her cheek
In her fair hand.

          And he, not able yet
To force himself away, and never more
Behold her, gathered blossom, primrose flowers,
And wild anemone, for many a clump
Grew all about him, and the hazel rods
Were nodding with their catkins.   But he heard
The stopping train, and felt that he must go ;
His time was come.   There was nought else to do

Or hope for. With the blossom he drew near,
And would have had her take it from his hand ;
But she, half lost in thought, held out her own,
And then remembering him and his long love,
She said, "I thank you ; pray you now forget,
Forget me, Laurance," and her lovely eyes
Softened ; but he was dumb, till through the trees
Suddenly broke upon their quietude
The woman and her child. And Muriel said,
"What will you ?" She made answer quick and keen,
"Your name, my lady ; 't is your name I want,
Tell me your name." Not startled, not displeased,
But with a musing sweetness on her mouth,
As if considering in how short a while
It would be changed, she lifted up her face
And gave it, and the little child drew near
And pulled her gown, and prayed her for the flowers.
Then Laurance, not content to leave them so,
Nor yet to wait the coming lover, spoke, —
"Your errand with this lady ?" — "And your right
To ask it ?" she broke out with sudden heat
And passion : "What is that to you ! Poor child !
Madam !" And Muriel lifted up her face
And looked, — they looked into each other's eyes.

"That man who comes," the clear-voiced woman cried,
"That man with whom you think to wed so soon,
You must not heed him. What ! the world is full

Of men, and some are good, and most, God knows,
Better than he, — that I should say it ! — far
Better." And down her face the large tears ran,
And Muriel's wild dilated eyes looked up,
Taking a terrible meaning from her words;
And Laurance stared about him half in doubt
If this were real, for all things were so blithe,
And soft air tossed the little flowers about ;
The child was singing, and the blackbirds piped,
Glad in fair sunshine. And the women both
Were quiet, gazing in each other's eyes.

He found his voice, and spoke: "This is not well,
Though whom you speak of should have done you wrong;
A man that could desert and plan to wed
Will not his purpose yield to God and right,
Only to law. You, whom I pity so much,
If you be come this day to urge a claim,
You will not tell me that your claim will hold;
'T is only, if I read aright, the old,
Sorrowful, hateful story !"
                          Muriel sighed,
With a dull patience that he marvelled at,
"Be plain with me. I know not what to think,
Unless you are his wife. Are you his wife?
Be plain with me." And all too quietly,
With running down of tears, the answer came,
"Ay, madam, ay ! the worse for him and me."
Then Muriel heard her lover's foot anear,

And cried upon him with a bitter cry,
Sharp and despairing. And those two stood back,
With such affright, and violent anger stirred
He broke from out the thicket to her side,
Not knowing. But, her hands before her face,
She sat; and, stepping close, that woman came
And faced him. Then said Muriel, " O my heart,
Herbert!" — and he was dumb, and ground his teeth,
And lifted up his hand and looked at it,
And at the woman; but a man was there
Who whirled her from her place, and thrust himself
Between them; he was strong, — a stalwart man:
And Herbert thinking on it, knew his name.
" What good," quoth he, " though you and I should strive
And wrestle all this April day? A word,
And not a blow, is what these women want:
Master yourself, and say it." But he, weak
With passion and great anguish, flung himself
Upon the seat and cried, " O lost, my love!
O Muriel, Muriel!" And the woman spoke,
" Sir, 't was an evil day you wed with me;
And you were young; I know it, sir, right well.
Sir, I have worked; I have not troubled you,
Not for myself, nor for your child. I know
We are not equal." " Hold! " he cried; " have done;
Your still, tame words are worse than hate or scorn.
Get from me! Ay, my wife, my wife, indeed!
All 's done. You hear it, Muriel; if you can,
O sweet, forgive me."

Then the woman moved
Slowly away : her little singing child
Went in her wake : and Muriel dropped her hands,
And sat before these two that loved her so,
Mute and unheeding.   There were angry words,
She knew, but yet she could not hear the words ;
And afterwards the man she loved stooped down
And kissed her forehead once, and then withdrew
To look at her, and with a gesture pray
Her pardon.   And she tried to speak, but failed,
And presently, and soon, O, — he was gone.

She heard him go, and Laurance, still as stone,
Remained beside her ; and she put her hand
Before her face again, and afterward
She heard a voice, as if a long way off,
Some one entreated, but she could not heed.
Thereon he drew her hand away, and raised
Her passive from her seat.   So then she knew
That he would have her go with him, go home, —
It was not far to go, — a dreary home.
A crippled aunt, of birth and lineage high,
Had in her youth, and for a place and home,
Married the stern old rector ; and the girl
Dwelt with them : she was orphaned, — had no kin
Nearer than they.   And Laurance brought her in,
And spared to her the telling of this woe.
He sought her kindred where they sat apart,
And laid before them all the cruel thing,

As he had seen it. After, he retired:
And restless, and not master of himself,
He day and night haunted the rectory lanes;
And all things, even to the spreading out
Of leaves, their flickering shadows on the ground,
Or sailing of the slow, white cloud, or peace
And glory and great light on mountain heads, —
All things were leagued against him, — ministered
By likeness or by contrast to his love.

But what was that to Muriel, though her peace
He would have purchased for her with all prayers,
And costly, passionate, despairing tears?
O what to her that he should find it worse
To bear her life's undoing than his own?

She let him see her, and she made no moan,
But talked full calmly of indifferent things,
Which when he heard, and marked the faded eyes
And lovely wasted cheek, he started up
With "This I cannot bear!" and shamed to feel
His manhood giving way, and utterly
Subdued by her sweet patience and his pain,
Made haste and from the window sprang, and paced,
Battling and chiding with himself, the maze.

She suffered, and he could not make her well
For all his loving; — he was naught to her.
And now his passionate nature, set astir,

Fought with the pain that could not be endured;
And like a wild thing suddenly aware
That it is caged, which flings and bruises all
Its body at the bars, he rose, and raged
Against the misery: then he made all worse
With tears.   But when he came to her again,
Willing to talk as they had talked before,
She sighed, and said, with that strange quietness,
" I know you have been crying": and she bent
Her own fair head and wept.
                                    She felt the cold —
The freezing cold that deadened all her life —
Give way a little; for this passionate
Sorrow, and all for her, relieved her heart,
And brought some natural warmth, some natural tears.

III.

And after that, though oft he sought her door,
He might not see her.   First they said to him,
" She is not well "; and afterwards, " Her wish
Is ever to be quiet."   Then in haste
They took her from the place, because so fast
She faded.   As for him, though youth and strength
Can bear the weight as of a world, at last
The burden of it tells, — he heard it said,
When autumn came, " The poor sweet thing will die:
That shock was mortal."   And he cared no more
To hide, if yet he could have hidden, the blight

E

That was laying waste his heart.   He journeyed south
To Devon, where she dwelt with other kin,
Good, kindly women ; and he wrote to them,
Praying that he might see her ere she died.

So in her patience she permitted him
To be about her, for it eased his heart ;
And as for her that was to die so soon,
What did it signify ?   She let him weep
Some passionate tears beside her couch, she spoke
Pitying words, and then they made him go,
It was enough they said, her time was short,
And he had seen her.   He HAD seen, and felt
The bitterness of death ; but he went home,
Being satisfied in that great longing now,
And able to endure what might befall.

    And Muriel lay, and faded with the year ;
She lay at the door of death, that opened not
To take her in ; for when the days once more
Began a little to increase, she felt, —
And it was sweet to her, she was so young, —
She felt a longing for the time of flowers,
And dreamed that she was walking in that wood
With her two feet among the primroses.

Then when the violet opened, she rose up
And walked : the tender leaf and tender light
Did solace her ; but she was white and wan,

The shadow of that Muriel, in the wood
Who listened to those deadly words.

     And now
Empurpled seas began to blush and bloom,
Doves made sweet moaning, and the guelder rose
In a great stillness dropped, and ever dropped,
Her wealth about her feet, and there it lay,
And drifted not at all. The lilac spread
Odorous essence round her ; and full oft,
When Muriel felt the warmth her pulses cheer,
She, faded, sat among the Maytide bloom,
And with a reverent quiet in her soul,
Took back — it was His will — her time, and sat
Learning again to live.
     Thus as she sat
Upon a day, she was aware of one
Who at a distance marked her. This again
Another day, and she was vexed, for yet
She longed for quiet ; but she heard a foot
Pass once again, and beckoned through the trees.
"Laurence!" And all impatient of unrest
And strife, ay, even of the sight of them,
When he drew near, with tired, tired lips,
As if her soul upbraided him, she said,
"Why have you done this thing?" He answered her,
"I am not always master in the fight :
I could not help it."
    "What!" she sighed, "not yet !
O, I am sorry"; and she talked to him

As one who looked to live, imploring him, —
"Try to forget me.　Let your fancy dwell
Elsewhere, nor me enrich with it so long ;
It wearies me to think of this your love.
Forget me ! "
　　　　　　He made answer, " I will try :
The task will take me all my life to learn,
Or were it learned, I know not how to live ;
This pain is part of life and being now, —
It is myself; but yet — but I will try."
Then she spoke friendly to him, — of his home,
His father, and the old, brave, loving folk ;
She bade him think of them.　And not her words,
But having seen her, satisfied his heart.
He left her, and went home to live his life,
And all the summer heard it said of her,
" Yet, she grows stronger "; but when autumn came
Again she drooped.
　　　　　　A bitter thing it is
To lose at once the lover and the love ;
For who receiveth not may yet keep life
In the spirit with bestowal.　But for her,
This Muriel, all was gone.　The man she loved,
Not only from her present had withdrawn,
But from her past, and there was no such man,
There never had been.
　　　　　　He was not as one
Who takes love in, like some sweet bird, and holds
The wingéd fluttering stranger to his breast,

Till, after transient stay, all unaware
It leaves him : it has flown.   No ; this may live
In memory, — loved till death.   He was not vile ;
For who by choice would part with that pure bird,
And lose the exaltation of its song ?
He had not strength of will to keep it fast,
Nor warmth of heart to keep it warm, nor life
Of thought to make the echo sound for him
After the song was done.   Pity that man :
His music is all flown, and he forgets
The sweetness of it, till at last he thinks
'T was no great matter.   But he was not vile,
Only a thing to pity most in man,
Weak, — only poor, and, if he knew it, undone.
But Herbert !   When she mused on it, her soul
Would fain have hidden him forevermore,
Even from herself: so pure of speech, so frank,
So full of household kindness.   Ah, so good
And true !   A little, she had sometimes thought,
Despondent for himself, but strong of faith
In God, and faith in her, this man had seemed.

Ay, he was gone ! and she whom he had wed,
As Muriel learned, was sick, was poor, was sad.
And Muriel wrote to comfort her, and send,
From her small store, money to help her need,
With, " Pray you keep it secret."   Then the whole
Of the cruel tale was told.

      What more ?   She died.

Her kin, profuse of thanks, not bitterly,
Wrote of the end. " Our sister fain had seen
Her husband ; prayed him sore to come.   But no.
And then she prayed him that he would forgive,
Madam, her breaking of the truth to you.
Dear madam, he was angry, yet we think
He might have let her see, before she died,
The words she wanted, but he did not write
Till she was gone — ' I neither can forgive,
Nor would I if I could.' "

                " Patience, my heart !
And this, then, is the man I loved ! "

                              But yet
He sought a lower level, for he wrote
Telling the story with a different hue,
Telling of freedom.   He desired to come,
" For now," said he, " O love, may all be well."
And she rose up against it in her soul,
For she despised him.   And with passionate tears
Of shame, she wrote, and only wrote these words, —
" Herbert, I will not see you."

                      Then she drooped
Again ; it is so bitter to despise ;
And all her strength, when autumn leaves down dropped,
Fell from her.   " Ah ! " she thought, " I rose up once,
I cannot rise up now ; here is the end."
And all her kinsfolk thought, " It is the end."

But when that other heard, " It is the end,"

His heart was sick, and he, as by a power
Far stronger than himself, was driven to her.
Reason rebelled against it, but his will
Required it of him with a craving strong
As life, and passionate though hopeless pain.

She, when she saw his face, considered him
Full quietly, let all excuses pass
Not answered, and considered yet again.

"He had heard that she was sick; what could he do
But come, and ask her pardon that he came?"
What could he do, indeed? — a weak white girl
Held all his heartstrings in her small white hand;
His youth, and power, and majesty were hers,
And not his own.
                    She looked, and pitied him,
Then spoke: "He loves me with a love that lasts.
Ah, me! that I might get away from it,
Or, better, hear it said that love IS NOT,
And then I could have rest.   My time is short,
I think, so short."   And roused against himself
In stormy wrath, that it should be his doom
Her to disquiet whom he loved; ay, her
For whom he would have given all his rest,
If there were any left to give; he took
Her words up bravely, promising once more
Absence, and praying pardon; but some tears
Dropped quietly upon her cheek.

                                                   " Remain,"
She said, " for there is something to be told,
Some words that you must hear.

                                       " And first hear this :
God has been good to me ; you must not think
That I despair.   There is a quiet time
Like evening in my soul.   I have no heart,
For cruel Herbert killed it long ago,
And death strides on.   Sit, then, and give your mind
To listen, and your eyes to look at me.
Look at my face, Laurance, how white it is ;
Look at my hand, — my beauty is all gone."
And Laurance lifted up his eyes ; he looked,
But answered, from their deeps that held no doubt,
Far otherwise than she had willed, — they said,
" Lovelier than ever."

                                   Yet her words went on,
Cold and so quiet, " I have suffered much,
And I would fain that none who care for me
Should suffer a like pang that I can spare.
Therefore," said she, and not at all could blush,
" I have brought my mind of late to think of this :
That since your life is spoilt (not willingly,
My God, not willingly by me), 't were well
To give you choice of griefs.

                                       " Were it not best
To weep for a dead love, and afterwards
Be comforted the sooner, that she died
Remote, and left not in your house and life

Aught to remind you? That indeed were best.
But were it best to weep for a dead wife,
And let the sorrow spend and satisfy
Itself with all expression, and so end?
I think not so; but if for you 't is best,
Then, — do not answer with too sudden words:
It matters much to you ; not much, not much
To me, — then truly I will die your wife ;
I will marry you."

           What was he like to say,
But, overcome with love and tears, to choose
The keener sorrow, — take it to his heart,
Cherish it, make it part of him, and watch
Those eyes that were his light till they should close?

He answered her with eager, faltering words,
"I choose, — my heart is yours, — die in my arms."

But was it well? Truly, at first, for him
It was not well: he saw her fade, and cried,
"When may this be?" She answered, "When you will,"
And cared not much, for very faint she grew,
Tired and cold. Oft in her soul she thought,
"If I could slip away before the ring
Is on my hand, it were a blessed lot
For both, — a blessed thing for him, and me."

But it was not so; for the day had come, —
Was over: days and months had come, and Death, —

4

Within whose shadow she had lain, which made
Earth and its loves, and even its bitterness,
Indifferent, — Death withdrew himself, and life
Woke up, and found that it was folded fast,
Drawn to another life forevermore.
O, what a waking! After it there came
Great silence. She got up once more, in spring,
And walked, but not alone, among the flowers.
She thought within herself, " What have I done ?
How shall I do the rest ? " And he, who felt
Her inmost thought, was silent even as she.
" What have we done ? " she thought. But as for him,
When she began to look him in the face,
Considering, " Thus and thus his features are,"
For she had never thought on them before,
She read their grave repose aright. She knew
That in the stronghold of his heart, held back,
Hidden reserves of measureless content
Kept house with happy thought, for her sake mute.

Most patient Muriel ! when he brought her home,
She took the place they gave her, — strove to please
His kin, and did not fail ; but yet thought on,
" What have I done ? how shall I do the rest ?
Ah ! so contented, Laurance, with this wife
That loves you not, for all the stateliness
And grandeur of your manhood, and the deeps
In your blue eyes." And after that awhile
She rested from such thinking, put it by

And waited.   She had thought on death before :
But no, this Muriel was not yet to die ;
And when she saw her little tender babe,
She felt how much the happy days of life
Outweigh the sorrowful.   A tiny thing,
Whom when it slept the lovely mother nursed
With reverent love, whom when it woke she fed
And wondered at, and lost herself in long
Rapture of watching, and contentment deep.

Once while she sat, this babe upon her knee,
Her husband and his father standing nigh,
About to ride, the grandmother, all pride
And consequence, so deep in learned talk
Of infants, and their little ways and wiles,
Broke off to say, " I never saw a babe
So like its father."   And the thought was new
To Muriel ; she looked up, and when she looked,
Her husband smiled.   And she, the lovely bloom
Flushing her face, would fain he had not known,
Nor noticed her surprise.   But he did know ;
Yet there was pleasure in his smile, and love
Tender and strong.   He kissed her, kissed his babe,
With " Goody, you are left in charge, take care " —
"As if I needed telling," quoth the dame ;
And they were gone.
                  Then Muriel, lost in thought,
Gazed ; and the grandmother, with open pride,
Tended the lovely pair ; till Muriel said,

"Is she so like? Dear granny, get me now
The picture that his father has"; and soon
The old woman put it in her hand.
　　　　　　　　　　　The wife,
Considering it with deep and strange delight,
Forgot for once her babe, and looked and learned.

A mouth for mastery and manful work,
A certain brooding sweetness in the eyes,
A brow the harbor of grave thought, and hair
Saxon of hue. She conned; then blushed again,
Remembering now, when she had looked on him,
The sudden radiance of her husband's smile.

But Muriel did not send the picture back;
She kept it; while her beauty and her babe
Flourished together, and in health and peace
She lived.
　　　　　　Her husband never said to her,
"Love, are you happy?" never said to her,
"Sweet, do you love me?" and at first, whene'er
They rode together in the lanes, and paused,
Stopping their horses, when the day was hot,
In the shadow of a tree, to watch the clouds,
Ruffled in drifting on the jagged rocks
That topped the mountains, — when she sat by him,
Withdrawn at even while the summer stars
Came starting out of nothing, as new made,
She felt a little trouble, and a wish

That he would yet keep silence, and he did.
That one reserve he would not touch, but still
Respected.
       Muriel grew more brave in time,
And talked at ease, and felt disquietude
Fade.   And another child was given to her.

"Now we shall do," the old great-grandsire cried,
"For this is the right sort, a boy."   "Fie, fie,"
Quoth the good dame; but never heed you, love,
He thinks them both as right as right can be."

But Laurance went from home, ere yet the boy
Was three weeks old.   It fretted him to go,
But yet he said, " I must ": and she was left
Much with the kindly dame, whose gentle care
Was like a mother's; and the two could talk
Sweetly, for all the difference in their years.

But unaware, the wife betrayed a wish
That she had known why Laurance left her thus.
"Ay, love," the dame made answer; "for he said,
'Goody,' before he left, 'if Muriel ask
No question, tell her naught; but if she let
Any disquietude appear to you,
Say what you know.' "   "What?" Muriel said, and
     laughed,
"I ask, then."
       " Child, it is that your old love,

Some two months past, was here.   Nay, never start :
He 's gone.   He came, our Laurance met him near ;
He said that he was going over seas,
'And might I see your wife this only once,
And get her pardon ? ' "

      " Mercy ! " Muriel cried,
" But Laurance does not wish it ? "

        " Nay, now, nay,"
Quoth the good dame.

     " I cannot," Muriel cried ;
" He does not, surely, think I should."

        " Not he,"
The kind old woman said, right soothingly.
" Does not he ever know, love, ever do
What you like best ? "

       And Muriel, trembling yet,
Agreed.   " I heard him say," the dame went on,
" For I was with him when they met that day,
'It would not be agreeable to my wife.' "

Then Muriel, pondering, — " And he said no more ?
You think he did not add, ' nor to myself ? ' "
And with her soft, calm, inward voice, the dame
Unruffled answered, " No, sweet heart, not he :
What need he care ? "   " And why not ? " Muriel cried,
Longing to hear the answer.   " O, he knows,
He knows, love, very well " : with that she smiled.
" Bless your fair face, you have not really thought
He did not know you loved him ? "

Muriel said,
"He never told me, goody, that he knew."
"Well," quoth the dame, "but it may chance, my dear,
That he thinks best to let old troubles sleep:
Why need to rouse them? You are happy, sure?
But if one asks, 'Art happy?' why, it sets
The thoughts a-working. No, say I, let love,
Let peace and happy folk alone.
                          "He said,
'It would not be agreeable to my wife.'
And he went on to add, in course of time
That he would ask you, when it suited you,
To write a few kind words."
                          "Yes," Muriel said,
"I can do that."
                    "So Laurance went, you see,"
The soft voice added, "to take down that child.
Laurance had written oft about the child,
And now, at last, the father made it known
He could not take him. He has lost, they say,
His money, with much gambling; now he wants
To lead a good, true, working life. He wrote,
And let this so be seen, that Laurance went
And took the child, and took the money down
To pay."
            And Muriel found her talking sweet,
And asked once more, the rather that she longed
To speak again of Laurance, "And you think
He knows I love him?"

"Ay, good sooth, he knows
No fear ; but he is like his father, love.
His father never asked my pretty child
One prying question ; took her as she was ;
Trusted her ; she has told me so : he knew
A woman's nature.   Laurance is the same.
He knows you love him ; but he will not speak ;
No, never.   Some men are such gentlemen !"

SONGS

OF

THE NIGHT WATCHES.

SONGS OF THE NIGHT WATCHES,

WITH AN INTRODUCTORY SONG OF EVENING, AND A
CONCLUDING SONG OF THE EARLY DAY.

———◆———

INTRODUCTORY.

(*Old English Manner.*)

APPRENTICED.

OME out and hear the waters shoot, the owlet
hoot, the owlet hoot;
   Yon crescent moon, a golden boat, hangs dim
behind the tree, O!
The dropping thorn makes white the grass, O sweetest
lass, and sweetest lass;
   Come out and smell the ricks of hay adown the croft
with me, O!"

" My granny nods before her wheel, and drops her reel,
and drops her reel;
   My father with his crony talks as gay as gay can
be, O!

But all the milk is yet to skim, ere light wax dim, ere
    light wax dim;
  How can I step adown the croft, my 'prentice lad, with
    thee, O?"

" And must ye bide, yet waiting 's long, and love is strong,
    and love is strong;
  And O! had I but served the time, that takes so long
    to flee, O!
And thou, my lass, by morning's light wast all in white,
    wast all in white,
  And parson stood within the rails, a-marrying me and
    thee, O."

THE FIRST WATCH.

TIRED.

I.

O, I WOULD tell you more, but I am tired;
  For I have longed, and I have had my will;
I pleaded in my spirit, I desired:
  " Ah! let me only see him, and be still
All my days after."
            Rock, and rock, and rock,
Over the falling, rising watery world,
  Sail, beautiful ship, along the leaping main;

The chirping land-birds follow flock on flock
  To light on a warmer plain.
White as weaned lambs the little wavelets curled,
    Fall over in harmless play,
    As these do far away;
Sail, bird of doom, along the shimmering sea,
All under thy broad wings that overshadow thee.

II.

    I am so tired,
If I would comfort me, I know not how,
  For I have seen thee, lad, as I desired,
And I have nothing left to long for now.

Nothing at all.   And did I wait for thee,
  Often and often, while the light grew dim,
And through the lilac branches I could see,
  Under a saffron sky, the purple rim
O' the heaving moorland?   Ay.   And then would float
Up from behind as it were a golden boat,
Freighted with fancies, all o' the wonder of life,
  Love — such a slender moon, going up and up,
Waxing so fast from night to night,
And swelling like an orange flower-bud, bright,
  Fated, methought, to round as to a golden cup,
And hold to my two lips life's best of wine.
  Most beautiful crescent moon,
      Ship of the sky!

Across the unfurrowed reaches sailing high.
  Methought that it would come my way full soon,
Laden with blessings that were all, all mine, —
  A golden ship, with balm and spiceries rife,
  That ere its day was done should hear thee call me wife.

III.

All over! the celestial sign hath failed ;
The orange flower-bud shuts ; the ship hath sailed,
  And sunk behind the long low-lying hills.
The love that fed on daily kisses dieth ;
The love kept warm by nearness, lieth
    Wounded and wan ;
  The love hope nourished bitter tears distils,
    And faints with naught to feed upon.
Only there stirreth very deep below
The hidden beating slow,
And the blind yearning, and the long-drawn breath
Of the love that conquers death.

IV.

Had we not loved full long, and lost all fear,
My ever, my only dear ?
Yes ; and I saw thee start upon thy way,
    So sure that we should meet
    Upon our trysting-day.
  And even absence then to me was sweet,

Because it brought me time to brood
Upon thy dearness in the solitude.
   But ah! to stay, and stay,
And let that moon of April wane itself away,
   And let the lovely May
Make ready all her buds for June;
And let the glossy finch forego her tune
That she brought with her in the spring,
And never more, I think, to me can sing;
And then to lead thee home another bride,
   In the sultry summertide,
And all forget me save for shame full sore,
That made thee pray me, absent, " See my face no more."

    v.

O hard, most hard! But while my fretted heart
  Shut out, shut down, and full of pain,
   Sobbed to itself apart,
   Ached to itself in vain,
   One came who loveth me
    As I love thee. . . . .
And let my God remember him for this,
As I do hope He will forget thy kiss,
  Nor visit on thy stately head
Aught that thy mouth hath sworn, or thy two eyes have
 said. . . . .
He came, and it was dark. He came, and sighed
Because he knew the sorrow, — whispering low,

And fast, and thick, as one that speaks by rote:
 " The vessel lieth in the river reach,
   A mile above the beach,
 And she will sail at the turning o' the tide."
   He said, " I have a boat,
   And were it good to go,
 And unbeholden in the vessel's wake
 Look on the man thou lovedst, and forgive,
 As he embarks, a shamefaced fugitive.
   Come, then, with me."

VI.

 O, how he sighed ! The little stars did wink,
 And it was very dark. I gave my hand, —
 He led me out across the pasture land,
   And through the narrow croft,
   Down to the river's brink.
When thou wast full in spring, thou little sleepy thing,
 The yellow flags that broidered thee would stand
 Up to their chins in water, and full oft
 WE pulled them and the other shining flowers,
   That all are gone to-day :
 WE two, that had so many things to say,
   So many hopes to render clear :
 And they are all gone after thee, my dear, —
   Gone after those sweet hours,
   That tender light, that balmy rain ;
   Gone " as a wind that passeth away,
   And cometh not again."

VII.

I only saw the stars, — I could not see
   The river, — and they seemed to lie
As far below as the other stars were high.
   I trembled like a thing about to die:
It was so awful 'neath the majesty
Of that great crystal height, that overhung
       The blackness at our feet,
       Unseen to fleet and fleet
       The flocking stars among,
   And only hear the dipping of the oar,
And the small wave's caressing of the darksome shore.

VIII.

   Less real it was than any dream.
Ah me! to hear the bending willows shiver,
As we shot quickly from the silent river,
   And felt the swaying and the flow
That bore us down the deeper, wider stream,
   Whereto its nameless waters go:
O! I shall always, when I shut mine eyes,
   See that weird sight again;
   The lights from anchored vessels hung;
   The phantom moon, that sprung
Suddenly up in dim and angry wise,
   From the rim o' the moaning main,
   And touched with elfin light

The two long oars whereby we made our flight,
   Along the reaches of the night;
Then furrowed up a lowering cloud,
   Went in, and left us darker than before,
To feel our way as the midnight watches wore,
And lie in HER lee, with mournful faces bowed,
That should receive and bear with her away
The brightest portion of my sunniest day, —
The laughter of the land, the sweetness of the shore.

IX.

And I beheld thee: saw the lantern flash
Down on thy face, when thou didst climb the side.
And thou wert pale, pale as the patient bride
   That followed; both a little sad,
Leaving of home and kin.   Thy courage glad,
   That once did bear thee on,
That brow of thine had lost; the fervor rash
Of unforeboding youth thou hadst foregone.
O, what a little moment, what a crumb
Of comfort for a heart to feed upon!
   And that was all its sum;
   A glimpse, and not a meeting, —
   A drawing near by night,
To sigh to thee an unacknowledged greeting,
And all between the flashing of a light
   And its retreating.

x.

Then after, ere she spread her wafting wings,
The ship, — and weighed her anchor to depart,
We stole from her dark lee, like guilty things;
    And there was silence in my heart,
And silence in the upper and the nether deep.
       O sleep! O sleep!
Do not forget me.   Sometimes come and sweep,
Now I have nothing left, thy healing hand
Over the lids that crave thy visits bland,
     Thou kind, thou comforting one :
    For I have seen his face, as I desired,
    And all my story is done.
     O, I am tired!

THE MIDDLE WATCH.

I.

I WOKE in the night, and the darkness was heavy and
       deep :
    I had known it was dark in my sleep,
      And I rose and looked out,
And the fathomless vault was all sparkling, set thick
      round about
With the ancient inhabiters silent, and wheeling too far

For man's heart, like a voyaging frigate, to sail, where
 remote
  In the sheen of their glory they float,
Or man's soul, like a bird, to fly near, of their beams to
 partake,
  And dazed in their wake,
  Drink day that is born of a star.
I murmured, " Remoteness and greatness, how deep you
 are set,
  How afar in the rim of the whole;
You know nothing of me, nor of man, nor of earth, O, nor
 yet
  Of our light-bearer, — drawing the marvellous moons
  as they roll,
  Of our regent, the sun.
I look on you trembling, and think, in the dark with my
 soul,
" How small is our place 'mid the kingdoms and nations
 of God:
  These are greater than we, every one."
And there falls a great fear, and a dread cometh over,
 that cries,
  " O my hope!   Is there any mistake?
Did He speak?   Did I hear?   Did I listen aright, if He
 spake?
Did I answer Him duly?   For surely I now am awake,
  If never I woke until now."
And a light, baffling wind, that leads nowhither, plays on
 my brow.

As a sleep, I must think on my day, of my path as un-
      trod,
Or trodden in dreams, in a dreamland whose coasts are a
      doubt ;
Whose countries recede from my thoughts, as they grope
      round about,
    And vanish, and tell me not how.
Be kind to our darkness, O Fashioner, dwelling in light,
    And feeding the lamps of the sky ;
Look down upon this one, and let it be sweet in Thy
      sight,
    I pray Thee, to-night.
O watch whom Thou madest to dwell on its soil, Thou
      Most High !
For this is a world full of sorrow (there may be but
      one) ;
Keep watch o'er its dust, else Thy children for aye are
      undone,
    For this is a world where we die.

II.

With that, a still voice in my spirit that moved and that
      yearned,
    (There fell a great calm while it spake,)
I had heard it erewhile, but the noises of life are so loud,
That sometimes it dies in the cry of the street and the
      crowd :
To the simple it cometh, — the child, or asleep, or awake,

And they know not from whence; of its nature the wise
never learned
By his wisdom; its secret the worker ne'er earned
By his toil; and the rich among men never bought with
his gold;
   Nor the times of its visiting monarchs controlled,
     Nor the jester put down with his jeers
   (For it moves where it will), nor its season the
aged discerned
     By thought, in the ripeness of years.

O elder than reason, and stronger than will!
   A voice, when the dark world is still:
Whence cometh it? Father Immortal, thou knowest!
and we, —
We are sure of that witness, that sense which is sent us
of Thee;
For it moves, and it yearns in its fellowship mighty and
dread,
And let down to our hearts it is touched by the tears that
we shed;
It is more than all meanings, and over all strife;
   On its tongue are the laws of our life,
   And it counts up the times of the dead.

III.

I will fear you, O stars, never more.
I have felt it! Go on, while the world is asleep,

Golden islands, fast moored in God's infinite deep.
Hark, hark to the words of sweet fashion, the harpings of
yore !
How they sang to Him, seer and saint, in the far away
lands :
" The heavens are the work of Thy hands ;
They shall perish, but Thou shalt endure ;
Yea, they all shall wax old, —
But Thy throne is established, O God, and Thy years are
made sure ;
They shall perish, but Thou shalt endure, —
They shall pass like a tale that is told."

Doth He answer, the Ancient of Days ?
Will He speak in the tongue and the fashion of
men ?
(Hist ! hist ! while the heaven-hung multitudes shine in
His praise,
His language of old.)   Nay, He spoke with them first ;
it was then
They lifted their eyes to His throne ;
" They shall call on Me, ' Thou art our Father, our God,
Thou alone ! '
For I made them, I led them in deserts and desolate
ways ;
I have found them a Ransom Divine ;
I have loved them with love everlasting, the children of
men ;
I swear by Myself, they are Mine."

THE MORNING WATCH.

THE COMING IN OF THE "MERMAIDEN."

THE moon is bleached as white as wool,
  And just dropping under;
Every star is gone but three,
  And they hang far asunder, —
There's a sea-ghost all in gray,
  A tall shape of wonder!

I am not satisfied with sleep, —
  The night is not ended.
But look how the sea-ghost comes,
  With wan skirts extended,
Stealing up in this weird hour,
  When light and dark are blended.

A vessel! To the old pier end
  Her happy course she's keeping;
I heard them name her yesterday:
  Some were pale with weeping;
Some with their heart-hunger sighed,
  She's in, — and they are sleeping.

O ! now with fancied greetings blest,
    They comfort their long aching :
The sea of sleep hath borne to them
    What would not come with waking,
And the dreams shall most be true
    In their blissful breaking.

The stars are gone, the rose-bloom comes, —
    No blush of maid is sweeter ;
The red sun, half way out of bed,
    Shall be the first to greet her.
None tell the news, yet sleepers wake,
    And rise, and run to meet her.

Their lost they have, they hold; from pain
    A keener bliss they borrow.
How natural is joy, my heart!
    How easy after sorrow !
For once, the best is come that hope
    Promised them " to-morrow."

CONCLUDING SONG OF DAWN.

(*Old English Manner.*)

A MORN OF MAY.

ALL the clouds about the sun lay up in golden
creases,
(Merry rings the maiden's voice that sings at dawn of
day ;)
Lambkins woke and skipped around to dry their dewy
fleeces,
So sweetly as she carolled, all on a morn of May.

Quoth the Sergeant, " Here I 'll halt ; here 's wine of joy
for drinking ;
To my heart she sets her hand, and in the strings doth
play ;
All among the daffodils, and fairer to my thinking,
And fresh as milk and roses, she sits this morn of May."

Quoth the Sergeant, " Work is work, but any ye might
make me,
If I worked for you, dear lass, I 'd count my holiday.
I 'm your slave for good and all, an' if ye will but take
me,
So sweetly as ye carol upon this morn of May."

"Medals count for worth," quoth she, "and scars are
    worn for honor;
But a slave an' if ye be, kind wooer, go your way."
All the nodding daffodils woke up and laughed upon her.
O! sweetly did she carol, all on that morn of May.

Gladsome leaves upon the bough, they fluttered fast and
    faster,
Fretting brook, till he would speak, did chide the dull
    delay:
" Beauty! when I said a slave, I think I meant a master;
So sweetly as ye carol all on this morn of May.

" Lass, I love you! Love is strong, and some men's
    hearts are tender."
Far she sought o'er wood and wold, but found not aught
    to say;
Mounting lark nor mantling cloud would any counsel
    render,
Though sweetly she had carolled upon that morn of May.

Shy, she sought the wooer's face, and deemed the wooing
    mended;
Proper man he was, good sooth, and one would have his
    way:
So the lass was made a wife, and so the song was ended.
O! sweetly she did carol all on that morn of May.

A STORY OF DOOM.

BOOK I.

NILOIYA said to Noah, "What aileth thee,
My master, unto whom is my desire,
The father of my sons?" He answered her,
"Mother of many children, I have heard
The Voice again." "Ah, me!" she saith, "ah, me!
What spake it?" Niloiya sighed.

This when the Master-builder heard, his heart
Was sad in him, the while he sat at home
And rested after toil. The steady rap
O' the shipwright's hammer sounding up the vale
Did seem to mock him; but her distaff down
Niloiya laid, and to the doorplace went,
Parted the purple covering seemly hung
Before it, and let in the crimson light
Of the descending sun. Then looked he forth, —
Looked, and beheld the hollow where the ark
Was a-preparing; where the dew distilled

All night from leaves of old lign aloe-trees,
Upon the gliding river; where the palm,
The almug, and the gophir shot their heads
Into the crimson brede that dyed the world:
And lo! he marked — unwieldy, dark, and huge —
The ship, his glory and his grief, — too vast
For that still river's floating, — building far
From mightier streams, amid the pastoral dells
Of shepherd kings.
        Niloiya spake again:
"What said the Voice, thou well-beloved man?"
He, laboring with his thought that troubled him,
Spoke on behalf of God: "Behold," said he,
"A little handful of unlovely dust
He fashioned to a lordly grace, and when
He laughed upon its beauty, it waxed warm,
And with His breath awoke a living soul.

"Shall not the Fashioner command His work?
And who am I, that, if He whisper, 'Rise,
Go forth upon Mine errand,' should reply,
'Lord, God, I love the woman and her sons, —
I love not scorning: I beseech Thee, God,
Have me excused.'"
        She answered him, "Tell on."
And he continuing, reasoned with his soul:
"What though I, — like some goodly lama sunk
In meadow grass, eating her way at ease,
Unseen of them that pass, and asking not

A wider prospect than of yellow-flowers
That nod above her head, — should lay me down,
And willingly forget this high behest,
There should be yet no tarrying.   Furthermore,
Though I went forth to cry against the doom,
Earth crieth louder, and she draws it down:
It hangeth balanced over us ; she crieth,
And it shall fall.   O ! as for me, my life
Is bitter, looking onward, for I know
That in the fulness of the time shall dawn
That day : my preaching shall not bring forth fruit,
Though for its sake I leave thee.   I shall float
Upon the abhorréd sea, that mankind hate,
With thee and thine."

      She answered : " God forbid !
For, sir, though men be evil, yet the deep
They dread, and at the last will surely turn
To Him, and He long-suffering will forgive,
And chide the waters back to their abyss,
To cover the pits where doleful creatures feed.
Sir, I am much afraid : I would not hear
Of riding on the waters : look you, sir,
Better it were to die with you by hand
Of them that hate us, than to live, ah me !
Rolling among the furrows of the unquiet,
Unconsecrate, unfriendly, dreadful sea."

He saith again : " I pray thee, woman, peace,
For thou wilt enter, when that day appears,

The fateful ship."

              " My lord," quoth she, " I will.
But O, good sir, be sure of this, be sure
The Master calleth ; for the time is long
That thou hast warned the world : thou art but here
Three days ; the song of welcoming but now
Is ended. I behold thee, I am glad ;
And wilt thou go again ? Husband, I say,
Be sure who 't is that calleth ; O, be sure,
Be sure. My mother's ghost came up last night,
Whilst I thy beard, held in my hands did kiss,
Leaning anear thee, wakeful through my love,
And watchful of thee till the moon went down.

" She never loved me since I went with thee
To sacrifice among the hills : she smelt
The holy smoke, and could no more divine
Till the new moon. I saw her ghost come up ;
It had a snake with a red comb of fire
Twisted about its waist, — the doggish head
Lolled on its shoulder, and so leered at me.
' This woman might be wiser,' quoth the ghost ;
' Shall there be husbands for her found below,
When she comes down to us ? O, fool ! O, fool !
She must not let her man go forth, to leave
Her desolate, and reap the whole world's scorn,
A harvest for himself.' With that they passed."

He said, " My crystal drop of perfectness,

I pity thee; it was an evil ghost:
Thou wilt not heed the counsel?" "I will not,"
Quoth she; "I am loyal to the Highest. Him
I hold by even as thou, and deem Him best.
Sir, am I fairer than when last we met?"

"God add," said he, "unto thy much yet more,
As I do think thou art." "And think you, sir,"
Niloiya saith, "that I have reached the prime?"
He answering, "Nay, not yet." "I would 't were so,"
She plaineth, "for the daughters mock at me:
Her locks forbear to grow, they say, so sore
She pineth for the master. Look you, sir,
They reach but to the knee. But thou art come,
And all goes merrier. Eat, my lord, of all
My supper that I set, and afterward
Tell me, I pray thee, somewhat of thy way;
Else shall I be despised as Adam was,
Who compassed not the learning of his sons,
But, grave and silent, oft would lower his head
And ponder, following of great Isha's feet,
When she would walk with her fair brow upraised,
Scorning the children that she bare to him."

"Ay," quoth the Master; "but they did amiss
When they despised their father: knowest thou that?"

"Sure he was foolisher," Niloiya saith,
"Than any that came after. Furthermore,

He had not heart nor courage for to rule :
He let the mastery fall from his slack hand.
Had not our glorious mother still borne up
His weakness, chid with him, and sat apart,
And listened, when the fit came over him
To talk on his lost garden, he had sunk
Into the slave of slaves."
    " Nay, thou must think
How he had dwelt long, God's loved husbandman,
And looked in hope among the tribes for one
To be his fellow, ere great Isha, once
Waking, he found at his left side, and knew
The deep delight of speech." So Noah, and thus
Added, " And therefore was his loss the more ;
For though the creatures he had singled out
His favorites, dared for him the fiery sword
And followed after him, — shall bleat of lamb
Console one for the foregone talk of God ?
Or in the afternoon, his faithful dog,
Fawning upon him, make his heart forget
At such a time, and such a time, to have heard
What he shall hear no more ?
    " O, as for him,
It was for this that he full oft would stop,
And, lost in thought, stand and revolve that deed,
Sad muttering, ' Woman ! we reproach thee not ;
Though thou didst eat mine immortality ;
Earth, be not sorry ; I was free to choose.
Wonder not, therefore, if he walked forlorn.

 5 *

Was not the helpmeet given to raise him up
From his contentment with the lower things?
Was she not somewhat that he could not rule
Beyond the action, that he could not have
By the mere holding, and that still aspired
And drew him after her?   So, when deceived
She fell by great desire to rise, he fell
By loss of upward drawing, when she took
An evil tongue to be her counsellor :
' Death is not as the death of lower things,
Rather a glorious change, begrudged of Heaven,
A change to being as gods,' — he from her hand,
Upon reflection, took of death that hour,
And ate it (not the death that she had dared) ;
He ate it knowing.   Then divisions came.
She, like a spirit strayed who lost the way,
Too venturesome, among the farther stars,
And hardly cares, because it hardly hopes
To find the path to heaven ; in bitter wise
Did bear to him degenerate seed, and he,
Once having felt her upward drawing, longed,
And yet aspired, and yearned to be restored,
Albeit she drew no more."

         " Sir, ye speak well,"
Niloiya saith, " but yet the mother sits
Higher than Adam.   He did understand
Discourse of birds and all four-footed things,
But she had knowledge of the many tribes
Of angels and their tongues ; their playful ways

And greetings when they met.   Was she not wise?
They say she knew much that she never told,
And had a voice that called to her as thou."

"Nay," quoth the Master-shipwright, "who am I
That I should answer?   As for me, poor man,
Here is my trouble: 'if there be a Voice,'
At first I cried, 'let me behold the mouth
That uttereth it.'   Thereon it held its peace.
But afterward, I, journeying up the hills,
Did hear it hollower than an echo fallen
Across some clear abyss; and I did stop,
And ask of all my company, 'What cheer?
If there be spirits abroad that call to us,
Sirs, hold your peace and hear.'   So they gave heed,
And one man said, 'It is the small ground-doves
That peck upon the stony hillocks': one,
'It is the mammoth in yon cedar swamp
That cheweth in his dream': and one, 'My lord,
It is the ghost of him that yesternight
We slew, because he grudged to yield his wife
To thy great father, when he peaceably
Did send to take her.'   Then I answered, 'Pass,'
And they went on; and I did lay mine ear
Close to the earth; but there came up therefrom
No sound, nor any speech; I waited long,
And in the saying, 'I will mount my beast
And on,' I was as one that in a trance
Beholdeth what is coming, and I saw

Great waters and a ship ; and somewhat spake,
' Lo, this shall be ; let him that heareth it,
And seeth it, go forth to warn his kind,
For I will drown the world.' "

Niloiya saith,
" Sir, was that all that ye went forth upon ? "
The master, he replieth, " Ay, at first,
That same was all ; but many days went by,
While I did reason with my heart and hope
For more, and struggle to remain, and think,
' Let me be certain ' ; and so think again,
' The counsel is but dark ; would I had more !
When I have more to guide me, I will go.'
And afterward, when reasoned on too much,
It seemed remoter, then I only said,
' O, would I had the same again ' ; and still
I had it not.

" Then at the last I cried,
' If the unseen be silent, I will speak
And certify my meaning to myself.
Say that He spoke, then He will make that good
Which He hath spoken.   Therefore it were best
To go, and do His bidding.   All the earth
Shall hear the judgment so, and none may cry
When the doom falls, " Thou God art hard on us ;
We knew not Thou wert angry.   O! we are lost,
Only for lack of being warned."

" ' But say
That He spoke not, and merely it befell

That I being weary had a dream.   Why, so
He could not suffer damage ; when the time
Was past, and that I threatened had not come,
Men would cry out on me, haply me kill,
For troubling their content.   They would not swear,
" God, that did send this man, is proved untrue,"
But rather, " Let him die ; he lied to us ;
God never sent him."   Only Thou, great King,
Knowest if Thou didst speak or no.   I leave
The matter here.   If Thou wilt speak again,
I go in gladness ; if Thou wilt not speak,
Nay, if Thou never didst, I not the less
Shall go, because I have believed, what time
I seemed to hear Thee, and the going stands
With memory of believing.'   Then I washed,
And did array me in the sacred gown,
And take a lamb."

                " Ay, sir," Niloiya sighed,
" I following, and I knew not anything
Till, the young lamb asleep in thy two arms,
We, moving up among the silent hills,
Paused in a grove to rest ; and many slaves
Came near to make obeisance, and to bring
Wood for the sacrifice, and turf and fire.
Then in their hearing thou didst say to me,
' Behold, I know thy good fidelity,
And theirs that are about us ; they would guard
The mountain passes, if it were my will
Awhile to leave thee ' ; and the pygmies laughed

For joy, that thou wouldst trust inferior things ;
And put their heads down, as their manner is,
To touch our feet. They laughed, but sore I wept ;
Sir, I could weep now ; ye did ill to go
If that was all your bidding ; I had thought
God drave thee, and thou couldst not choose but go."

Then said the son of Lamech, " Afterward,
When I had left thee, He whom I had served
Met with me in the visions of the night,
To comfort me for that I had withdrawn
From thy dear company. He sware to me
That no man should molest thee, no, nor touch
The bordering of mine outmost field. I say,
When I obeyed, He made His matters plain.
With whom could I have left thee, but with them,
Born in thy mother's house, and bound thy slaves ?"

She said, " I love not pygmies ; they are naught."
And he, " Who made them pygmies ?" Then she pushed
Her veiling hair back from her round, soft eyes,
And answered, wondering, " Sir, my mothers did,
Ye know it." And he drew her near to sit
Beside him on the settle, answering, " Ay."
And they went on to talk as writ below,
If any one shall read :
                    " Thy mother did,
And they that went before her. Thinkest thou
That they did well ? "

      " They had been overcome ;
And when the angered conquerors drave them out,
Behoved them find some other way to rule, —
They did but use their wits.   Hath not man aye
Been cunning in dominion, among beasts
To breed for size or swiftness, or for sake
Of the white wool he loveth, at his choice ?
What harm if coveting a race of men
That could but serve, they sought among their thralls,
Such as were low of stature, men and maids ;
Ay, and of feeble will and quiet mind ?
Did they not spend much gear to gather out
Such as I tell of, and for matching them
One with another for a thousand years ?
What harm, then, if there came of it a race,
Inferior in their wits, and in their size,
And well content to serve ? "

                  " ' What harm ? ' thou sayest.
My wife doth ask, ' What harm ? ' "

                     " Your pardon, sir.
I do remember that there came one day,
Two of the grave old angels that God made,
When first He invented life (right old they were,
And plain, and venerable) ; and they said,
Rebuking of my mother as with hers
She sat, ' Ye do not well, you wives of men,
To match your wit against the Maker's will,
And for your benefit to lower the stamp
Of His fair image, which He set at first

Upon man's goodly frame ; ye do not well
To treat his likeness even as ye treat
The bird and beast that perish.' "

     " Said they aught
To appease the ancients, or to speak them fair ? "

" How know I ?   'T was a slave that told it me.
My mother was full old when I was born,
And that was in her youth.   What think you, sir ?
Did not the giants likewise ill ? "

      " To that
I have no answer ready.   If a man,
When each one is against his fellow, rule,
Or unmolested dwell, or unreproved,
Because, for size and strength, he standeth first,
He will thereof be glad ; and if he say,
' I will to wife choose me a stately maid,
And leave a goodly offspring ' ; 'sooth, I think,
He sinneth not ; for good to him and his
He would be strong and great.   Thy people's fault
Was, that for ill to others, they did plot
To make them weak and small."

      " But yet they steal
Or take in war the strongest maids, and such
As are of highest stature ; ay, and oft
They fight among themselves for that same cause.
And they are proud against the King of heaven :
They hope in course of ages they shall come
To be as strong as He."

The Master said,
"I will not hear thee talk thereof; my heart
Is sick for all this wicked world.   Fair wife,
I am right weary.   Call thy slaves to thee,
And bid that they prepare the sleeping place.
O would that I might rest !   I fain would rest,
And, no more wandering, tell a thankless world
My never-heeded tale !"
      With that she called.
The moon was up, and some few stars were out,
While heavy at the heart he walked abroad
To meditate before his sleep.   And yet
Niloiya pondered, " Shall my master go?
And will my master go?   What 'vaileth it,
That he doth spend himself, over the waste
A wandering, till he reach outlandish folk,
That mock his warning?   O, what 'vaileth it,
That he doth lavish wealth to build yon ark,
Whereat the daughters, when they eat with me,
Laugh?   O my heart ! I would the Voice were stilled.
Is not he happy?   Who, of all the earth,
Obeyed like to me?   Have not I learned
From his dear mouth to utter seemly words,
And lay the powers my mother gave me by?
Have I made offerings to the dragon?   Nay,
And I am faithful, when he leaveth me
Lonely betwixt the peakéd mountain tops
In this long valley, where no stranger foot
Can come without my will.   He shall not go.

Not yet, not yet! But three days — only three —
Beside me, and a muttering on the third,
'I have heard the Voice again.' Be dull, O dull,
Mind and remembrance! Mother, ye did ill;
'T is hard unlawful knowledge not to use.
Why, O dark mother! opened ye the way?"
Yet when he entered, and did lay aside
His costly robe of sacrifice, the robe
Wherein he had been offering, ere the sun
Went down; forgetful of her mother's craft,
She lovely and submiss did mourn to him:
" Thou wilt not go, — I pray thee, do not go,
Till thou hast seen thy children." And he said,
" I will not. I have cried, and have prevailed:
To-morrow it is given me by the Voice
Upon a four days' journey to proceed,
And follow down the river, till its waves
Are swallowed in the sand, where no flesh dwells.

" ' There,' quoth the Unrevealèd, ' we shall meet,
And I will counsel thee; and thou shalt turn
And rest thee with the mother, and with them
She bare.' Now, therefore, when the morn appears,
Thou fairest among women, call thy slaves,
And bid them yoke the steers, and spread thy car
With robes, the choicest work of cunning hands;
Array thee in thy rich apparel, deck
Thy locks with gold; and while the hollow vale
I thread beside yon river, go thou forth

Atween the mountains to my father's house,
And let thy slaves make all obeisance due,
And take and lay an offering at his feet.
Then light, and cry to him, ' Great king, the son
Of old Methuselah, thy son hath sent
To fetch the growing maids, his children, home.' "

" Sir," quoth the woman, " I will do this thing,
So thou keep faith with me, and yet return.
But will the Voice, think you, forbear to chide,
Nor that Unseen, who calleth, buffet thee,
And drive thee on ? "

        He saith, " It will keep faith.
Fear not. I have prevailed, for I besought,
And lovingly it answered. I shall rest,
And dwell with thee till after my three sons
Come from the chase." She said, " I let them forth
In fear, for they are young. Their slaves are few.
The giant elephants be cunning folk ;
They lie in ambush, and will draw men on
To follow, — then will turn and tread them down."
" Thy father's house unwisely planned," said he,
" To drive them down upon the growing corn
Of them that were their foes ; for now, behold,
They suffer while the unwieldy beasts delay
Retirement to their lands, and, meanwhile, pound
The damp, deep meadows, to a pulpy mash ;
Or wallowing in the waters foul them ; nay,
Tread down the banks, and let them forth to flood

Their cities ; or, assailed and falling, shake
The walls, and taint the wind, ere thirty men,
Over the hairy terror piling stones
Or earth, prevail to cover it."

　　　　　　　　　She said,
" Husband, I have been sorry, thinking oft
I would my sons were home ; but now so well
Methinks it is with me, that I am fain
To wish they might delay, for thou wilt dwell
With me till after they return, and thou
Hast set thine eyes upon them.   Then, — ah, me !
I must sit joyless in my place ; bereft,
As trees that suddenly have dropped their leaves,
And dark as nights that have no moon."

　　　　　　　　　She spake :
The hope o' the world did hearken, but reply
Made none.   He left his hand on her fair locks
As she lay sobbing ; and the quietness
Of night began to comfort her, the fall
Of far-off waters, and the wingéd wind
That went among the trees.   The patient hand,
Moreover, that was steady, wrought with her,
Until she said, " What wilt thou ?   Nay, I know.
I therefore answer what thou utterest not.
Thou lovest me well, and not for thine own will
Consentest to depart.   What more ?   Ay, this :
I do avow that He which calleth thee,
Hath right to call ; and I do swear, the Voice
Shall have no let of me, to do Its will."

BOOK II.

NOW ere the sunrise, while the morning star
    Hung yet behind the pine bough, woke and prayed
The world's great shipwright, and his soul was glad
Because the Voice was favorable. Now
Began the tap o' the hammer, now ran forth
The slaves preparing food. They therefore ate
In peace together; then Niloiya forth
Behind the milk-white steers went on her way;
And the great Master-builder, down the course
Of the long river, on his errand sped,
And as he went, he thought:

                [They do not well
Who, walking up a trodden path, all smooth
With footsteps of their fellows, and made straight
From town to town, will scorn at them that wonn
Under the covert of God's eldest trees
(Such as He planted with His hand, and fed
With dew before rain fell, till they stood close
And awful; drank the light up as it dropt,
And kept the dusk of ages at their roots);
They do not well who mock at such, and cry,
" We peaceably, without or fault or fear,
Proceed, and miss not of our end; but these
Are slow and fearful: with uncertain pace,
And ever reasoning of the way, they oft,

After all reasoning, choose the worser course,
And plunged in swamp, or in the matted growth
Nigh smothered struggle, all to reach a goal
Not worth their pains." Nor do they well whose work
Is still to feed and shelter them and theirs,
Get gain, and gathered store it, to think scorn
Of those who work for a world (no wages paid
By a Master hid in light), and sent alone
To face a laughing multitude, whose eyes
Are full of damaging pity, that forbears
To tell the harmless laborer, " Thou art mad."]

And as he went, he thought : " They counsel me,
Ay, with a kind of reason in their talk,
' Consider; call thy soberer thought to aid ;
Why to but one man should a message come ?
And why, if but to one, to thee ? Art thou
Above us, greater, wiser ? Had He sent,
He had willed that we should heed. Then since He
          knoweth
That such as thou, a wise man cannot heed,
He did not send.' My answer, ' Great and wise,
If He had sent with thunder, and a voice
Leaping from heaven, ye must have heard ; but so
Ye had been robbed of choice, and, like the beasts,
Yoked to obedience. God makes no men slaves.'
They tell me, ' God is great above thy thought :
He meddles not : and this small world is ours,
These many hundred years we govern it ;

Old Adam, after Eden, saw Him not.'
Then I, ' It may be He is gone to knead
More clay.   But look, my masters ; one of you
Going to warfare, layeth up his gown,
His sickle, or his gold, and thinks no more
Upon it, till young trees have waxen great ;
At last, when he returneth, he will seek
His own.   And God, shall He not do the like ?
And having set new worlds a-rolling, come
And say, " I will betake Me to the earth
That I did make ": and having found it vile,
Be sorry.   Why should man be free, you wise,
And not the Master ? '   Then they answer, ' Fool !
A man shall cast a stone into the air
For pastime, or for lack of heed, — but He !
Will He come fingering of His ended work,
Fright it with His approaching face, or snatch
One day the rolling wonder from its ring,
And hold it quivering, as a wanton child
Might take a nestling from its downy bed,
And having satisfied a careless wish,
Go thrust it back into its place again ? '
To such I answer, and, that doubt once mine,
I am assured that I do speak aright :
' Sirs, the significance of this your doubt
Lies in the reason of it ; ye do grudge
That these your lands should have another Lord ;
Ye are not loyal, therefore ye would fain
Your King would bide afar.   But if ye looked

For countenance and favor when He came,
Knowing yourselves right worthy, would ye care,
With cautious reasoning, deep and hard, to prove
That He would never come, and would your wrath
Be hot against a prophet?   Nay, I wot
That as a flatterer you would look on him, —
" Full of sweet words thy mouth is: if He come, —
We think not that He will, — but if He come,
Would it might be to-morrow, or to-night,
Because we look for praise." ' "

                        Now, as he went,
The noontide heats came on, and he grew faint ;
But while he sat below an almug-tree,
A slave approached with greeting.   " Master, hail ! "
He answered, " Hail ! what wilt thou ? "   Then she said,
" The palace of thy fathers standeth nigh."
" I know it," quoth he ; and she said again,
" The Elder, learning thou wouldst pass, hath sent
To fetch thee " ; then he rose and followed her.
So first they walked beneath a lofty roof
Of living bough and tendril, woven on high
To let no drop of sunshine through, and hung
With gold and purple fruitage, and the white
Thick cups of scented blossom.   Underneath,
Soft grew the sward and delicate, and flocks
Of egrets, ay, and many cranes, stood up,
Fanning their wings, to agitate and cool
The noonday air, as men with heed and pains
Had taught them, marshalling and taming them
To bear the wind in, on their moving wings.

So long time as a nimble slave would spend
In milking of her cow, they walked at ease;
Then reached the palace, all of forest trunks,
Brought whole, and set together, made. Therein
Had dwelt old Adam, when his mighty sons
Had finished it, and up to Eden gate
Had journeyed for to fetch him. "Here," they said,
"Mother and father, ye may dwell, and here
Forget the garden wholly."
              So he came
Under the doorplace, and the women sat,
Each with her finger on her lips; but he,
Having been called, went on, until he reached
The jewelled settle, wrought with cunning work
Of gold and ivory, whereon they wont
To set the Elder. All with sleekest skins,
That striped and spotted creatures of the wood
Had worn, the seat was covered, but thereon
The Elder was not; by the steps thereof,
Upon the floor, whereto his silver beard
Did reach, he sat, and he was in his trance.
Upon the settle many doves were perched,
That set the air a going with their wings:
These opposite, the world's great shipwright stood
To wait the burden; and the Elder spake:
"Will He forget me? Would He might forget!
Old, old! The hope of old Methuselah
Is all in His forgetfulness." With that,
A slave-girl took a cup of wine, and crept

6

Anear him, saying, " Taste "; and when his lips
Had touched it, lo, he trembled, and he cried,
" Behold, I prophesy."

              Then straight they fled
That were about him, and did stand apart
And stop their ears.   For he, from time to time,
Was plagued with that same fate to prophesy,
And spake against himself, against his day
And time, in words that all men did abhor.
Therefore, he warning them what time the fit
Came on him, saved them, that they heard it not.
So while they fled, he cried: " I saw the God
Reach out of heaven His wonderful right hand.
Lo, lo! He dipped it in the unquiet sea,
And in its curvéd palm behold the ark,
As in a vast calm lake, came floating on.
Ay, then, His other hand — the cursing hand —
He took and spread between us and the sun,
And all was black ; the day was blotted out,
And horrible staggering took the frighted earth.
I heard the water hiss, and then methinks
The crack as of her splitting.   Did she take
Their palaces that are my brothers dear,
And huddle them with all their ancientry
Under into her breast ?   If it was black,
How could this old man see ?   There was a noise
I' the dark, and He drew back His hand again.
I looked, — It was a dream, — let no man say
It was aught else.   There, so — the fit goes by.

Sir, and my daughters, is it eventide? —
Sooner than that, saith old Methuselah,
Let the vulture lay his beak to my green limbs.
What! art Thou envious? — are the sons of men
Too wise to please Thee, and to do Thy will?
Methuselah, he sitteth on the ground,
Clad in his gown of age, the pale white gown,
And goeth not forth to war; his wrinkled hands
He claspeth round his knees: old, very old.
Would he could steal from Thee one secret more —
The secret of Thy youth! O, envious God!
We die. The words of old Methuselah
And his prophecy are ended."

                    Then the wives,
Beholding how he trembled, and the maids
And children, came anear, saying, " Who art thou
That standest gazing on the Elder? Lo,
Thou dost not well: withdraw; for it was thou
Whose stranger presence troubled him, and brought
The fit of prophecy." And he did turn
To look upon them, and their majesty
And glorious beauty took away his words;
And being pure among the vile, he cast
In his thought a veil of snow-white purity
Over the beauteous throng. " Thou dost not well,"
They said. He answered: " Blossoms o' the world,
Fruitful as fair, never in watered glade,
Where in the youngest grass blue cups push forth,
And the white lily reareth up her head,

And purples cluster, and the saffron flower
Clear as a flame of sacrifice breaks out,
And every cedar bough, made delicate
With climbing roses, drops in white and red, —
So I (good angels keep you in their care)
So beautiful a crowd."

                With that, they stamped,
Gnashed their white teeth, and turning, fled and spat
Upon the floor. The Elder spake to him,
Yet shaking with the burden, "Who art thou?"
He answered, "I, the man whom thou didst send
To fetch through this thy woodland, do forbear
To tell my name; thou lovest it not, great sire, —
No, nor mine errand. To thy house I spake,
Touching their beauty." "Wherefore didst thou spite,"
Quoth he, "the daughters?" and it seemed he lost
Count of that prophecy, for very age,
And from his thin lips dropt a trembling laugh.
"Wicked old man," quoth he, "this wise old man
I see as 't were not I. Thou bad old man,
What shall be done to thee? for thou didst burn
Their babes, and strew the ashes all about,
To rid the world of His white soldiers. Ay,
Scenting of human sacrifice, they fled.
Cowards! I heard them winnow their great wings:
They went to tell Him; but they came no more.
The women hate to hear of them, so sore
They grudged their little ones; and yet no way
There was but that. I took it; I did well."

With that he fell to weeping. "Son," said he,
"Long have I hid mine eyes from stalwart men,
For it is hard to lose the majesty
And pride and power of manhood: but to-day,
Stand forth into the light, that I may look
Upon thy strength, and think, EVEN THUS DID I,
IN THE GLORY OF MY YOUTH, MORE LIKE TO GOD
THAN LIKE HIS SOLDIERS, FACE THE VASSAL WORLD."

Then Noah stood forward in his majesty,
Shouldering the golden billhook, wherewithal
He wont to cut his way, when tangled in
The matted hayes. And down the opened roof
Fell slanting beams upon his stately head,
And streamed along his gown, and made to shine
The jewelled sandals on his feet.
                    And, lo,
The Elder cried aloud: "I prophesy.
Behold, my son is as a fruitful field
When all the lands are waste. The archers drew, —
They drew the bow against him; they were fain
To slay: but he shall live, — my son shall live,
And I shall live by him in the other days.
Behold the prophet of the Most High God:
Hear him. Behold the hope o' the world, what time
She lieth under. Hear him; he shall save
A seed alive, and sow the earth with man.
O, earth! earth! earth! a floating shell of wood
Shall hold the remnant of thy mighty lords.

Will this old man be in it?   Sir, and you
My daughters, hear him!   Lo, this white old man
He sitteth on the ground.   (Let be, let be:
Why dost Thou trouble us to make our tongue
Ring with abhorréd words?)   The prophecy
Of the Elder, and the vision that he saw,
They both are ended."

                         Then said Noah: " The life
Of this my lord is low for very age:
Why then, with bitter words upon thy tongue,
Father of Lamech, dost thou anger Him?
Thou canst not strive against Him now."   He said:
" Thy feet are toward the valley, where lie bones
Bleaching upon the desert.   Did I love
The lithe strong lizards that I yoked and set
To draw my car? and were they not possessed?
Yea, all of them were liars.   I loved them well.
What did the Enemy, but on a day
When I behind my talking team went forth,
They sweetly lying, so that all men praised
Their flattering tongues and mild persuasive eyes, —
What did the Enemy but send His slaves,
Angels, to cast down stones upon their heads
And break them?   Nay, I could not stir abroad
But havoc came ; they never crept or flew
Beyond the shelter that I builded here.
But straight the crowns I had set upon their heads
Were marks for myrmidons that in the clouds
Kept watch to crush them.   Can a man forgive

That hath been warred on thus? I will not. Nay,
I swear it, — I, the man Methuselah."
The Master-shipwright, he replied, " 'T is true,
Great loss was that; but they that stood thy friends,
The wicked spirits, spoke upon their tongues,
And cursed the God of heaven. What marvel, sir,
If He was angered?" But the Elder cried,
" They all are dead, — the toward beasts I loved;
My goodly team, my joy, they all are dead;
Their bones lie bleaching in the wilderness:
And I will keep my wrath for evermore
Against the Enemy that slew them. Go,
Thou coward servant of a tyrant King,
Go down the desert of the bones, and ask,
' My King, what bones are these? Methuselah,
The white old man that sitteth on the ground,
Sendeth a message, " Bid them that they live,
And let my lizards run up every path
They wont to take when out of silver pipes,
The pipes that Tubal wrought into my roof,
I blew a sweeter cry than song-bird's throat
Hath ever formed; and while they laid their heads
Submiss upon my threshold, poured away
Music that welled by heartsful out, and made
The throats of men that heard to swell, their breasts
To heave with the joy of grief; yea, caused the lips
To laugh of men asleep.
                              Return to me
The great wise lizards; ay, and them that flew

My pursuivants before me.   Let me yoke
Again that multitude ; and here I swear
That they shall draw my car and me thereon
Straight to the ship of doom.   So men shall know
My loyalty, that I submit, and Thou
Shalt yet have honor, O mine Enemy,
By me.   The speech of old Methuselah."'"
Then Noah made answer, "By the living God,
That is no enemy to men, great sire,
I will not take thy message ; hear thou Him.
'Behold (He saith that suffereth thee), behold,
The earth that I made green cries out to Me,
Red with the costly blood of beauteous man.
I am robbed, I am robbed (He saith) ; they sacrifice
To evil demons of My blameless flocks,
That I did fashion with My hand.   Behold,
How goodly was the world!   I gave it thee
Fresh from its finishing.   What hast thou done ?
I will cry out to the waters, *Cover it,*
And hide it from its Father.   Lo, Mine eyes
Turn from it shamed.' "
                              With that the old man laughed
Full softly.   "Ay," quoth he, "a goodly world,
And we have done with it as we did list.
Why did He give it us ?   Nay, look you, son :
Five score they were that died in yonder waste ;
And if He crieth, 'Repent, be reconciled,'
I answer, 'Nay, my lizards'; and again,
If He will trouble me in this mine age,

'Why hast Thou slain my lizards?' Now my speech
Is cut away from all my other words,
Standing alone. The Elder sweareth it,
The man of many days, Methuselah."
Then answered Noah, "My Master, hear it not;
But yet have patience"; and he turned himself,
And down betwixt the ordered trees went forth,
And in the light of evening made his way
Into the waste to meet the Voice of God.

BOOK III.

ABOVE the head of great Methuselah
There lay two demons in the opened roof
Invisible, and gathered up his words;
For when the Elder prophesied, it came
About, that hidden things were shown to them,
And burdens that he spake against his time.

(But never heard them, such as dwelt with him;
Their ears they stopped, and willed to live at ease
In all delight; and perfect in their youth,
And strong, disport them in the perfect world.)

Now these were fettered that they could not fly,
For a certain disobedience they had wrought
Against the ruler of their host; but not
The less they loved their cause; and when the feet
O' the Master-builder were no longer heard,
They, slipping to the sward, right painfully
Did follow, for the one to the other said,
" Behoves our master know of this; and us,
Should he be favorable, he may loose
From these our bonds."

                    And thus it came to pass,
That while at dead of night the old dragon lay
Coiled in the cavern where he dwelt, the watch

Pacing before it saw in middle air
A boat, that gleamed like fire, and on it came,
And rocked as it drew near, and then it burst
And went to pieces, and there fell therefrom,
Close at the cavern's mouth, two glowing balls.

Now there was drawn a curtain nigh the mouth
Of that deep cave, to testify of wrath.
The dragon had been wroth with some that served,
And chased them from him ; and his oracles,
That wont to drop from him, were stopped, and men
Might only pray to him through that fell web
That hung before him.   Then did whisper low
Some of the little spirits that bat-like clung
And clustered round the opening.   " Lo," they said,
While gazed the watch upon those glowing balls,
" These are like moons eclipsed ; but let them lie
Red on the moss, and sear its dewy spires,
Until our lord give leave to draw the web,
And quicken reverence by his presence dread,
For he will know and call to them by name,
And they will change.   At present he is sick,
And wills that none disturb him."   So they lay,
And there was silence, for the forest tribes
Came never near that cave.   Wiser than men,
They fled the serpent hiss that oft by night
Came forth of it, and feared the wan dusk forms
That stalked among the trees, and in the dark
Those whiffs of flame that wandered up the sky

And made the moonlight sickly.

               Now, the cave
Was marvellous for beauty, wrought with tools
Into the living rock, for there had worked
All cunning men, to cut on it with signs
And shows, yea, all the manner of mankind.
The fateful apple-tree was there, a bough
Bent with the weight of him that us beguiled ;
And lilies of the field did seem to blow
And bud in the storied stone. There Tubal sat,
Who from his harp delivered music, sweet
As any in the spheres. Yea, more ;
Earth's latest wonder, on the walls appeared,
Unfinished, workmen clustering on its ribs ;
And farther back, within the rock hewn out,
Angelic figures stood, that impious hands
Had fashioned ; many golden lamps they held
By golden chains depending, and their eyes
All tended in a reverend quietude
Toward the couch whereon the dragon lay.
The floor was beaten gold ; the curly lengths
Of his last coils lay on it, hid from sight
With a coverlet made stiff with crusting gems,
Fire opals shooting, rubies, fierce bright eyes
Of diamonds, or the pale green emerald,
That changed their lustre when he breathed.

                   His head
Feathered with crimson combs, and all his neck,
And half-shut fans of his admiréd wings,

That in their scaly splendor put to shame
Or gold or stone, lay on his ivory couch
And shivered; for the dragon suffered pain:
He suffered and he feared. It was his doom,
The tempter, that he never should depart
From the bright creature that in Paradise
He for his evil purpose erst possessed,
Until it died. Thus only, spirit of might
And chiefest spirit of ill, could he be free.

But with its nature wed, as souls of men
Are wedded to their clay, he took the dread
Of death and dying, and the coward heart
Of the beast, and craven terrors of the end
Sank him that habited within it to dread
Disunion. He, a dark dominion erst
Rebellious, lay and trembled, for the flesh
Daunted his immaterial. He was sick
And sorry. Great ones of the earth had sent
Their chief musicians for to comfort him,
Chanting his praise, the friend of man, the god
That gave them knowledge, at so great a price
And costly. Yea, the riches of the mine,
And glorious broidered work, and woven gold,
And all things wisely made, they at his feet
Laid daily; for they said, " This mighty one,
All the world wonders after him. He lieth
Sick in his dwelling; he hath long foregone
(To do us good) dominion, and a throne,

And his brave warfare with the Enemy,
So much he pitieth us that were denied
The gain and gladness of this knowledge. Now
Shall he be certified of gratitude,
And smell the sacrifice that most he loves."

The night was dark, but every lamp gave forth
A tender, lustrous beam.   His beauteous wings
The dragon fluttered, cursed awhile, then turned
And moaned with lamentable voice, " I thirst,
Give me to drink."   Thereon stepped out in haste,
From inner chambers, lovely ministrants,
Young boys, with radiant locks and peaceful eyes,
And poured out liquor from their cups, to cool
His parchèd tongue, and kneeling held it nigh
In jewelled basins sparkling ; and he lapped,
And was appeased, and said, " I will not hide
Longer, my much desired face from men.
Draw back the web of separation."   Then
With cries of gratulation ran they forth,
And flung it wide, and all the watch fell low,
Each on his face, as drunk with sudden joy.
Thus marked he, glowing on the branchèd moss,
Those red rare moons, and let his serpent eyes
Consider them full subtly, " What be these ? "
Enquiring : and the little spirits said,
" As we for thy protection (having heard
That wrathful sons of darkness walk to-night,
Such as do oft ill use us), clustered here,

We marked a boat a-fire that sailed the skies,
And furrowed up like spray a billowy cloud,
And, lo, it went to pieces, scattering down
A rain of sparks and these two angry moons."
Then said the dragon, " Let my guard, and you,
Attendant hosts, recede"; and they went back,
And formed about the cave a widening ring,
Then halting, stood afar ; and from the cave
The snaky wonder spoke, with hissing tongue,
" If ye were Tartis and Deleisonon,
Be Tartis and Deleisonon once more."

Then egg-like cracked the glowing balls, and forth
Started black angels, trampling hard to free
Their fettered feet from out the smoking shell.

And he said, " Tartis and Deleisonon,
Your lord I am : draw nigh." " Thou art our lord,"
They answered, and with fettered limbs full low
They bent, and made obeisance. Furthermore,
" O fiery flying serpent, after whom
The nations go, let thy dominion last,"
They said, " forever." And the serpent said,
" It shall : unfold your errand." They replied,
One speaking for a space, and afterward
His fellow taking up the word with fear
And panting, " We were set to watch the mouth
Of great Methuselah. There came to him
The son of Lamech two days since. My lord,

They prophesied, the Elder prophesied,
Unwitting, of the flood of waters, — ay,
A vision was before him, and the lands
Lay under water drowned : he saw the ark, —
It floated in the Enemy's right hand."
Lord of the lost, the son of Lamech fled
Into the wilderness to meet His voice
That reigneth ; and we, diligent to hear
Aught that might serve thee, followed, but, forbid
To enter, lay upon its boundary cliff,
And wished for morning.

    " When the dawn was red,
We sought the man, we marked him ; and he prayed, —
Kneeling, he prayed in the valley, and he said — "
" Nay," quoth the serpent, " spare me, what devout
He fawning grovelled to the All-powerful ;
But if of what shall hap he aught let fall,
Speak that." They answered, " He did pray as one
That looketh to outlive mankind, — and more,
We are certified by all his scattered words,
That HE will take from men their length of days,
And cut them off like grass in its first flower :
From henceforth this shall be."

     That when he heard,
The dragon made to the night his moan.

      " And more,"
They said, " that He above would have men know
That He doth love them, whoso will repent,
To that man he is favorable, yea,

Will be his loving Lord."
      The dragon cried,
"The last is worse than all. O, man, thy heart
Is stout against His wrath. But will He love?
I heard it rumored in the heavens of old,
(And doth He love?) Thou wilt not, canst not, stand
Against the love of God. Dominion fails;
I see it float from me, that long have worn
Fetters of flesh to win it. Love of God!
I cry against thee; thou art worse than all."
They answered, " Be not moved, admiréd chief
And trusted of mankind"; and they went on,
And fed him with the prophecies that fell
From the Master-shipwright in his prayer.
        But prone

He lay, for he was sick : at every word
Prophetic cowering. As a bruising blow,
It fell upon his head and daunted him,
Until they ended, saying, " Prince, behold,
Thy servants have revealed the whole."
         Thereon

He out of snaky lips did hiss forth thanks.
Then said he, " Tartis and Deleisonon,
Receive your wages." So their fetters fell;
And they retiring, landed him, and cried,
" King, reign forever." Then he mourned, "Amen."

And he, — being left alone, — he said: " A light!
I see a light, — a star among the trees, —

An angel." And it drew toward the cave,
But with its sacred feet touched not the grass,
Nor lifted up the lids of its pure eyes,
But hung a span's length from that ground pollute,
At the opening of the cave.

     And when he looked,
The dragon cried, " Thou newly-fashioned thing,
Of name unknown, thy scorn becomes thee not.
Doth not thy Master suffer what thine eyes
Thou countest all too clean to open on?"
But still it hovered, and the quietness
Of holy heaven was on the drooping lids;
And not as one that answereth, it let fall
The music from its mouth, but like to one
That doth not hear, or, hearing, doth not heed.

" A message: ' I have heard thee, while remote
I went My rounds among the unfinished stars.'
A message: ' I have left thee to thy ways,
And mastered all thy vileness, for thy hate
I have made to serve the ends of My great love.
Hereafter will I chain thee down. To-day
One thing thou art forbidden; now thou knowest
The name thereof: I told it thee in heaven,
When thou wert sitting at My feet. Forbear
To let that hidden thing be whispered forth:
For man, ungrateful (and thy hope it was,
That so ungrateful he might prove), would scorn,
And not believe it, adding so fresh weight

Of condemnation to the doomèd world.
Concerning that, thou art forbid to speak ;
Know thou didst count it, falling from My tongue,
A lovely song, whose meaning was unknown,
Unknowable, unbearable to thought,
But sweeter in the hearing than all harps
Toned in My holy hollow.   Now thine ears
Are opened, know it, and discern and fear,
Forbearing speech of it for evermore.'"

So said, it turned, and with a cry of joy,
As one released, went up : and it was dawn,
And all boughs dropped with dew, and out of mist
Came the red sun and looked into the cave.

But the dragon, left a-tremble, called to him,
From the nether kingdom, certain of his friends, —
Three whom he trusted, councillors accursed.
A thunder-cloud stooped low and swathed the place
In its black swirls, and out of it they rushed,
And hid them in recesses of the cave,
Because they could not look upon the sun,
Sith light is pure.   And Satan called to them, —
All in the dark, in his great rage he spake :
" Up," quoth the dragon ; " it is time to work,
Or we are all undone."   And he did hiss,
And there came shudderings over land and trees,
A dimness after dawn.   The earth threw out
A blinding fog, that crept toward the cave,

And rolled up blank before it like a veil, —
A curtain to conceal its habiters.
Then did those spirits move upon the floor,
Like pillars of darkness, and with eyes aglow.
One had a helm for covering of the scars
That seamed what rested of a goodly face;
He wore his vizor up, and all his words
Were hollower than an echo from the hills:
He was hight Make.   And, lo, his fellow-fiend
Came after, holding down his dastard head,
Like one ashamed: now this for craft was great;
The dragon honored him.   A third sat down
Among them, covering with his wasted hand
Somewhat that pained his breast.

                           And when the fit
Of thunder, and the sobbings of the wind,
Were lulled, the dragon spoke with wrath and rage,
And told them of his matters: " Look to this,
If ye be loyal"; adding, " Give your thoughts,
And let me have your counsel in this need."

One spirit rose and spake, and all the cave
Was full of sighs, " The words of Make the Prince,
Of him once delegate in Betelgeux:
Whereas of late the manner is to change,
We know not where 't will end; and now my words
Go thus: give way, be peaceable, lie still
And strive not, else the world that we have won
He may, to drive us out, reduce to nought.

" For while I stood in mine obedience yet,
Steering of Betelgeux my sun, behold,
A moon, that evil ones did fill, rolled up
Astray, and suddenly the Master came,
And while, a million strong, like rooks they rose,
He took and broke it, flung it here and there,
And called a blast to drive the powder forth ;
And it was fine as dust, and blurred the skies
Farther than 't is from hence to this young sun.
Spirits that passed upon their work that day,
Cried out, ' How dusty 't is.'   Behoves us, then,
That we depart, as leaving unto Him
This goodly world and goodly race of man.
Not all are doomed ; hereafter it may be
That we find place on it again.   But if,
Too zealous to preserve it, and the men
Our servants, we oppose Him, He may come
And choosing rather to undo His work
Than strive with it for aye, make so an end."

He sighing paused.   Lo, then the serpent hissed
In impotent rage, " Depart ! and how depart !
Can flesh be carried down where spirits wonn ?
Or I, most miserable, hold my life
Over the airless, bottomless gulf, and bide
The buffetings of yonder shoreless sea ?
O death, thou terrible doom : O death, thou dread
Of all that breathe."

               A spirit rose and spake ;

" Whereas in Heaven is power, is much to fear ;
For this admiréd country we have marred.
Whereas in Heaven is love (and there are days
When yet I can recall what love was like),
Is naught to fear.　A threatening makes the whole,
And clogged with strong conditions :　' O, repent,
Man, and I turn.'　He, therefore, powerful now,
And more so, master, that ye bide in clay,
Threateneth that He may save.　They shall not die."

The dragon said, " I tremble, I am sick."
He said with pain of heart, " How am I fallen !
For I keep silence ; yea, I have withdrawn
From haunting of His gates, and shouting up
Defiance.　Wherefore doth He hunt me out
From this small world, this little one, that I
Have been content to take unto myself,
I here being loved and worshippéd ?　He knoweth
How much I have foregone ; and must He stoop
To whelm the world, and heave the floors o' the deep,
Of purpose to pursue me from my place ?
And since I gave men knowledge, must He take
Their length of days whereby they perfect it ?
So shall He scatter all that I have stored,
And get them by degrading them.　I know
That in the end it is appointed me
To fade.　I will not fade before the time."

A spirit rose, the third, a spirit ashamed

And subtle, and his face he turned aside :
" Whereas," said he, " we strive against both power
And love, behoves us that we strive aright.
Now some of old my comrades, yesterday
I met, as they did journey to appear
In the Presence ; and I said, ' My master lieth
Sick yonder, otherwise (for no decree
There stands against it) he would also come
And make obeisance with the sons of God.'
They answered, naught denying.   Therefore, lord,
'T is certain that ye have admittance yet ;
And what doth hinder ?   Nothing but this breath.
Were it not well to make an end, and die,
And gain admittance to the King of kings ?
What if thy slaves by thy consent should take
And bear thee on their wings above the earth,
And suddenly let fall, — how soon 't were o'er !
We should have fear and sinking at the heart ;
But in a little moment we should see,
Rising majestic from a ruined heap,
The stately spirit that we served of yore."

The serpent turned his subtle deadly eyes
Upon the spirit, and hissed ; and sick with shame,
It bowed itself together, and went back
With hidden face.   " This counsel is not good,"
The other twain made answer ; " look, my lord,
Whereas 't is evil in thine eyes, in ours
'T is evil also ; speak, for we perceive

That on thy tongue the words of counsel sit,
Ready to fly to our right greedy ears,
That long for them." And Satan, flattered thus
(Forever may the serpent kind be charmed,
With soft sweet words, and music deftly played),
Replied, " Whereas I surely rule the world,
Behoves that ye prepare for me a path,
And that I, putting of my pains aside,
Go stir rebellion in the mighty hearts
O' the giants ; for He loveth them, and looks
Full oft complacent on their glorious strength.
He willeth that they yield, that He may spare ;
But, by the blackness of my loathed den,
I say they shall not, no, they shall not yield ;
Go, therefore, take to you some harmless guise,
And spread a rumor that I come. I, sick,
Sorry, and aged, hasten. I have heard
Whispers that out of heaven dropped unaware.
I caught them up, and sith they bode men harm,
I am ready for to comfort them ; yea, more,
To counsel, and I will that they drive forth
The women, the abhorréd of my soul ;
Let not a woman breathe where I shall pass,
Lest the curse falleth, and she bruise my head.
Friends, if it be their mind to send for me
An army, and triumphant draw me on
In the golden car ye wot of, and with shouts,
I would not that ye hinder them. Ah, then
Will I make hard their hearts, and grieve Him sore,

That loves them, O, by much too well to wet
Their stately heads, and soil those locks of strength
Under the fateful brine.   Then afterward,
'While He doth reason vainly with them, I
Will offer Him a pact: ' Great King, a pact,
And men shall worship Thee, I say they shall,
For I will bid them do it, yea, and leave
To sacrifice their kind, so Thou my name
Wilt suffer to be worshipped after Thine.' "

" Yea, my lord Satan," quoth they, " do this thing,
And let us hear thy words, for they are sweet."

Then he made answer, " By a messenger
Have I this day been warned.   There is a deed
I may not tell of, lest the people add
Scorn to a Coming Greatness to their faults.
Why this ?   Who careth when about to slay,
And slay indeed, how well they have deserved
Death, whom he slayeth ?   Therefore yet is hid
A meaning of some mercy that will rob
The nether world.   Now look to it, — 'T were vain
Albeit this deluge He would send indeed,
That we expect the harvest ; He would yet
Be the Master-reaper ; for I heard it said,
They that be young and know Him not, and they
That are bound and may not build, yea, more, their wives,
Whom, suffering not to hear the doom, they keep
Joyous behind the curtains, every one

7   J

With maidens nourished in the house, and babes
And children at her knees, — (then what remain !)
He claimeth and will gather for His own.
Now, therefore, it were good by guile to work,
Princes, and suffer not the doom to fall.
There is no evil like to love.   I heard
Him whisper it.   Have I put on this flesh
To ruin his two children beautiful,
And shall my deed confound me in the end,
Through awful imitation ?   Love of God,
I cry against thee ; thou art worst of all."

BOOK IV.

NOW while these evil ones took counsel strange,
 The son of Lamech journeyed home ; and, lo !
A company came down, and struck the track
As he did enter it. There rode in front
Two horsemen, young and noble, and behind
Were following slaves with tent gear ; others led
Strong horses, others bare the instruments
O' the chase, and in the rear dull camels lagged,
Sighing, for they were burdened, and they loved
The desert sands above that grassy vale.

And as they met, those horsemen drew the rein,
And fixed on him their grave untroubled eyes ;
He in his regal grandeur walked alone,
And had nor steed nor follower, and his mien
Was grave and like to theirs. He said to them,
" Fair sirs, whose are ye ? " They made answer cold,
" The beautiful woman, sir, our mother dear,
Niloiya, bear us to great Lamech's son."
And he, replying, " I am he." They said,
" We know it, sir. We have remembered you
Through many seasons. Pray you let us not ;
We fain would greet our mother." And they made
Obeisance and passed on ; then all their train,
Which while they spoke had halted, moved apace,

And, while the silent father stood, went by,
He gazing after, as a man that dreams ;
For he was sick with their cold, quiet scorn,
That seemed to say, " Father, we own you not,
We love you not, for you have left us long, —
So long, we care not that you come again."

And while the sullen camels moved, he spake
To him that led the last, " There are but two
Of these my sons ; but where doth Japhet ride ?
For I would see him."   And the leader said,
" Sir, ye shall find him, if ye follow up
Along the track.   Afore the noonday meal
The young men, even our masters, bathed ; (there grows
A clump of cedars by the bend of yon
Clear river) — there did Japhet, after meat,
Being right weary, lay him down and sleep.
There, with a company of slaves and some
Few camels, ye shall find him."
                              And the man
The father of these three, did let him pass,
And struggle and give battle to his heart,
Standing as motionless as pillar set
To guide a wanderer in a pathless waste ;
But all his strength went from him, and he strove
Vainly to trample out and trample down
The misery of his love unsatisfied, —
Unutterable love flung in his face.

Then he broke out in passionate words, that cried
Against his lot, " I have lost my own, and won
None other ; no, not one !   Alas, my sons !
That I have looked to for my solacing,
In the bitterness to come.   My children dear ! "
And when from his own lips he heard those words,
With passionate stirring of the heart, he wept.

And none came near to comfort him.   His face
Was on the ground ; but, having wept, he rose
Full hastily, and urged his way to find
The river ; and in hollow of his hand
Raised up the water to his brow : " This son,
This other son of mine," he said, " shall see
No tears upon my face."   And he looked on,
Beheld the camels, and a group of slaves
Sitting apart from some one fast asleep,
Where they had spread out webs of broidery work
Under a cedar-tree ; and he came on,
And when they made obeisance he declared
His name, and said, " I will beside my son
Sit till he wakeneth."   So Japhet lay
A-dreaming, and his father drew to him.
He said, " This cannot scorn me yet "; and paused,
Right angry with himself, because the youth,
Albeit of stately growth, so languidly
Lay with a listless smile upon his mouth,
That was full sweet and pure ; and as he looked,
He half forgot his trouble in his pride.

"And is this mine?" said he, "my son! mine own!
(God, thou art good!)   O, if this turn away,
That pang shall be past bearing.   I must think
That all the sweetness of his goodly face
Is copied from his soul.   How beautiful
Are children to their fathers!   Son, my heart
Is greatly glad because of thee; my life
Shall lack of no completeness in the days
To come.   If I forget the joy of youth,
In thee shall I be comforted; ay, see
My youth, a dearer than my own again."

And when he ceased, the youth, with sleep content,
Murmured a little, turned himself and woke.

He woke, and opened on his father's face
The darkness of his eyes; but not a word
The Master-shipwright said, — his lips were sealed;
He was not ready, for he feared to see
This mouth curl up with scorn.   And Japhet spoke,
Full of the calm that cometh after sleep:
"Sir, I have dreamed of you.   I pray you, sir,
What is your name?" and even with his words
His countenance changed.   The son of Lamech said,
"Why art thou sad?   What have I done to thee?"
And Japhet answered, "O, methought I fled
In the wilderness before a maddened beast,
And you came up and slew it; and I thought
You were my father; but I fear me, sir,

My thoughts were vain." With that his father said,
" Whate'er of blessing Thou reserv'st for me,
God! if Thou wilt not give to both, give here :
Bless him with both Thy hands "; and laid his own
On Japhet's head.
     Then Japhet looked on him,
Made quiet by content, and answered low,
With faltering laughter, glad and reverent : " Sir,
You are my father ? " " Ay," quoth he, " I am !
Kiss me, my son ; and let me hear my name,
My much desiréd name, from your dear lips."

Then after, rested, they betook them home :
And Japhet, walking by the Master, thought,
" I did not will to love this sire of mine ;
But now I feel as if I had always known
And loved him well ; truly, I see not why,
But I would rather serve him than go free
With my two brethren." And he said to him,
" Father ! " — who answered, " I am here, my son."
And Japhet said, " I pray you, sir, attend
To this my answer : let me go with you,
For, now I think on it, I do not love
The chase, nor managing the steed, nor yet
The arrows and the bow ; but rather you,
For all you do and say, and you yourself,
Are goodly and delightsome in mine eyes.
I pray you, sir, when you go forth again,
That I may also go." And he replied,

" I will tell thy speech unto the Highest; He
Shall answer it.   But I would speak to thee
Now of the days to come.   Know thou, most dear
To this thy father, that the drenchéd world,
When risen clean washed from water, shall receive
From thee her lordliest governors, from thee
Daughters of noblest soul."
                 So Japhet said,
" Sir, I am young, but of my mother straight
I will go ask a wife, that this may be.
I pray you, therefore, as the manner is
Of fathers, give me land that I may reap
Corn for sustaining of my wife, and bruise
The fruit of the vine to cheer her."   But he said,
" Dost thou forget? or dost thou not believe,
My son?"   He answered, "I did ne'er believe,
My father, ere to-day; but now, methinks,
Whatever thou believest I believe,
For thy belovéd sake.   If this then be
As thou (I hear) hast said, and earth doth bear
The last of her wheat harvests, and make ripe
The latest of her grapes; yet hear me, sir,
None of the daughters shall be given to me
If I be landless."   Then his father said,
" Lift up thine eyes toward the north, my son"
And so he did.   " Behold thy heritage!"
Quoth the world's prince and master, " far away
Upon the side o' the north, where green the field
Lies every season through, and where the dews

Of heaven are wholesome, shall thy children reign ;
I part it to them, for the earth is mine ;
The Highest gave it me :   I make it theirs.
Moreover, for thy marriage gift, behold
The cedars where thou sleepedst !   There are vines ;
And up the rise is growing wheat.   I give
(For all, alas ! is mine), — I give thee both
For dowry, and my blessing."
And he said,
" Sir, you are good, and therefore the Most High
Shall bless me also.   Sir, I love you well."

7 *

BOOK V.

AND when two days were over, Japhet said,
    " Mother, so please you, get a wife for me."
The mother answered, " Dost thou mock me, son ?
'T is not the manner of our kin to wed
So young.   Thou knowest it ; art thou not ashamed ?
Thou carest not for a wife."   And the youth blushed,
And made for answer : " This, my father, saith
The doom is nigh ; now therefore find a maid,
Or else shall I be wifeless all my days.
And as for me, I care not ; but the lands
Are parted, and the goodliest share is mine.
And lo ! my brethren are betrothed ; their maids
Are with thee in the house.   Then why not mine ?
Didst thou not diligently search for these
Among the noblest born of all the earth,
And bring them up ?   My sisters, dwell they not
With women that bespake them for their sons ?
Now, therefore, let a wife be found for me,
Fair as the day, and gentle to my will
As thou art to my father's."   When she heard,
Niloiya sighed, and answered, " It is well."
And Japhet went out from her presence.

                                 Then
Quoth the great Master : " Wherefore sought ye not,
Woman, these many days, nor tired at all,

Till ye had found, a maiden for my son?
In this ye have done ill." Niloiya said:
" Let not my lord be angry. All my soul
Is sad : my lord hath walked afar so long,
That some despise thee ; yea, our servants fail
Lately to bring their stint of corn and wood.
And, sir, thy household slaves do steal away
To thy great father, and our lands lie waste, —
None till them : therefore think the women scorn
To give me, — whatsoever gems I send,
And goodly raiment, — (yea, I seek afar,
And sue with all desire and humbleness
Through every master's house, but no one gives) —
A daughter for my son." With that she ceased.

Then said the Master : " Some thou hast with thee,
Brought up among thy children, dutiful
And fair ; thy father gave them for my slaves, —
Children of them whom he brought captive forth
From their own heritage." And she replied,
Right scornfully : " Shall Japhet wed a slave ? "
Then said the Master : " He shall wed : look thou
To that. I say not he shall wed a slave ;
But by the might of One that made him mine,
I will not quit thee for my doomèd way
Until thou wilt betroth him. Therefore, haste,
Beautiful woman, loved of me and mine,
To bring a maiden, and to say, ' Behold
A wife for Japhet.' " Then she answered, " Sir,

It shall be done."

              And forth Niloiya sped.
She gathered all her jewels, — all she held
Of costly or of rich, — and went and spake
With some few slaves that yet abode with her,
For daily they were fewer ; and went forth,
With fair and flattering words, among her feres,
And fain had wrought with them : and she had hope
That made her sick, it was so faint ; and then
She had fear, and after she had certainty,
For all did scorn her. " Nay," they cried, " O fool !
If this be so, and on a watery world
Ye think to rock, what matters if a wife
Be free or bond ? There shall be none to rule,
If she have freedom : if she have it not,
None shall there be to serve."

              And she alit,
The time being done, desponding at her door,
And went behind a screen, where should have wrought
The daughters of the captives ; but there wrought
One only, and this rose from off the floor,
Where she the river rush full deftly wove,
And made obeisance. Then Niloiya said,
" Where are thy fellows ?" And the maid replied,
" Let not Niloiya, this my lady loved,
Be angry ; they are fled since yesternight."
Then said Niloiya, " Amarant, my slave,
When have I called thee by thy name before ? "
She answered, " Lady, never "; and she took

And spread her broidered robe before her face.
Niloiya spoke thus : " I am come to woe,
And thou to honor."   Saying this, she wept
Passionate tears ; and all the damsel's soul
Was full of yearning wonder, and her robe
Slipped from her hand, and her right innocent face
Was seen betwixt her locks of tawny hair
That dropped about her knees, and her two eyes,
Blue as the much-loved flower that rims the beck,
Looked sweetly on Niloiya ; but she knew
No meaning in her words ; and she drew nigh,
And kneeled and said, " Will this my lady speak ?
Her damsel is desirous of her words."
Then said Niloiya, " I, thy mistress, sought
A wife for Japhet, and no wife is found."
And yet again she wept with grief of heart,
Saying, " Ah me, miserable ! I must give
A wife : the Master willeth it : a wife,
Ah me ! unto the high-born.   He will scorn
His mother and reproach me.   I must give —
None else have I to give — a slave, — even thee."
This further spake Niloiya : " I was good, —
Had rue on thee, a tender sucking child,
When they did tear thee from thy mother's breast ;
I fed thee, gave thee shelter, and I taught
Thy hands all cunning arts that women prize.
But out on me ! my good is turned to ill.
O, Japhet, well-beloved ! "   And she rose up,
And did restrain herself, saying, " Dost thou heed ?

Behold, this thing shall be." The damsel sighed,
"Lady, I do." Then went Niloiya forth.

And Amarant murmured in her deep amaze,
" Shall Japhet's little children kiss my mouth ?
And will he sometimes take them from my arms,
And almost care for me for their sweet sake ?
I have not dared to think I loved him, — now
I know it well : but O, the bitterness
For him !" And ending thus, the damsel rose,
For Japhet entered. And she bowed herself
Meekly and made obeisance, but her blood
Ran cold about her heart, for all his face
Was colored with his passion.
                                        Japhet spoke :
He said, " My father's slave"; and she replied,
Low drooping her fair head, " My master's son."
And after that a silence fell on them,
With trembling at her heart, and rage at his.
And Japhet, mastered of his passion, sat
And could not speak. O ! cruel seemed his fate, —
So cruel her that told it, so unkind.
His breast was full of wounded love and wrath
Wrestling together ; and his eyes flashed out
Indignant lights, as all amazed he took
The insult home that she had offered him,
Who should have held his honor dear.
                                        And, lo,
The misery choked him and he cried in pain,

" Go, get thee forth "; but she, all white and still,
Parted her lips to speak, and yet spake not,
Nor moved. And Japhet rose up passionate,
With lifted arm as one about to strike ;
But she cried out and met him, and she held
With desperate might his hand, and prayed to him,
" Strike not, or else shall men from henceforth say,
' Japhet is like to us.' " And he shook off
The damsel, and he said, " I thank thee, slave ;
For never have I stricken yet or child
Or woman. Not for thy sake am I glad,
Nay, but for mine. Get hence. Obey my words."
Then Japhet lifted up his voice, and wept.

And no more he restrained himself, but cried,
With heavings of the heart, " O hateful day !
O day that shuts the door upon delight.
A slave ! to wed a slave ! O loathéd wife,
Hated of Japhet's soul." And after, long,
With face between his hands, he sat, his thoughts
Sullen and sore; then scorned himself, and saying,
" I will not take her, I will die unwed,
It is but that "; lift up his eyes and saw
The slave, and she was sitting at his feet ;
And he, so greatly wondering that she dared
The disobedience, looked her in the face
Less angry than afraid, for pale she was
As lily yet unsmiled on by the sun ;
And he, his passion being spent, sighed out,

"Low am I fallen indeed.   Hast thou no fear,
That thou dost flout me?" but she gave to him
The sighing echo of his sigh, and mourned,
" No."

       And he wondered, and he looked again,
For in her heart there was a new-born pang,
That cried ; but she, as mothers with their young,
Suffered, yet loved it ; and there shone a strange
Grave sweetness in her blue unsullied eyes.
And Japhet, leaning from the settle, thought,
" What is it ?   I will call her by her name,
To comfort her, for also she is naught
To blame ; and since I will not her to wife,
She falls back from the freedom she had hoped."
Then he said " Amarant"; and the damsel drew
Her eyes down slowly from the shaded sky
Of even, and she said, " My master's son,
Japhet"; and Japhet said, " I am not wroth
With thee, but wretched for my mother's deed,
Because she shamed me."

       And the maiden said,
" Doth not thy father love thee well, sweet sir ?"
" Ay," quoth he, " well."   She answered, " Let the heart
Of Japhet, then, be merry.   Go to him
And say, ' The damsel whom my mother chose,
Sits by her in the house ; but as for me,
Sir, ere I take her, let me go with you
To that same outland country.   Also, sir,
My damsel hath not worked as yet the robe

Of her betrothal'; now, then, sith he loves,
He will not say thee nay.   Herein for awhile
Is respite, and thy mother far and near
Will seek again : it may be she will find
A fair, free maiden."

         Japhet said, " O maid,
Sweet are thy words ; but what if I return,
And all again be as it is to-day ?"
Then Amarant answered, " Some have died in youth ;
But yet, I think not, sir, that I shall die.
Though ye shall find it even as I had died, —
Silent, for any words I might have said ;
Empty, for any space I might have filled.
Sir, I will steal away, and hide afar ;
But if a wife be found, then will I bide
And serve."   He answered, " O, thy speech is good ;
Now therefore (since my mother gave me thee),
I will reward it ; I will find for thee
A goodly husband, and will make him free
Thee also."

        Then she started from his feet,
And, red with shame and anger, flashed on him
The passion of her eyes ; and put her hands
With catching of the breath to her fair throat,
And stood in her defiance lost to fear,
Like some fair hind in desperate danger turned·
And brought to bay, and wild in her despair.
But shortly, " I remember," quoth she, low,
With raining down of tears and broken sighs,

                                        K

"That I am Japhet's slave; beseech you, sir,
As ye were ever gentle, ay, and sweet
Of language to me, be not harder now.
Sir, I was yours to take; I knew not, sir,
That also ye might give me.   Pray you, sir,
Be pitiful, — be merciful to me,
A slave."   He said, "I thought to do thee good,
For good hath been thy counsel"; but she cried,
"Good master, be you therefore pitiful
To me, a slave."   And Japhet wondered much
At her, and at her beauty, for he thought,
"None of the daughters are so fair as this,
Nor stand with such a grace majestical;
She in her locks is like the travelling sun,
Setting, all clad in coiling clouds of gold.
And would she die unmatched?"   He said to her,
"What! wilt thou sail alone in yonder ship,
And dwell alone hereafter?"   "Ay," she said,
"And serve my mistress."

                                    "It is well," quoth he,
And held his hand to her, as is the way
Of masters.   Then she kissed it, and she said,
"Thanks for benevolence," and turned herself,
Adding, "I rest, sir, on your gracious words";
Then stepped into the twilight and was gone.

And Japhet, having found his father, said,
"Sir, let me also journey when ye go."
Who answered, "Hath thy mother done her part?"

He said, " Yea, truly, and my damsel sits
Before her in the house ; and also, sir,
She said to me, ' I have not worked, as yet,
The garment of betrothal.' "   And he said,
" 'T is not the manner of our kin to speak
Concerning matters that a woman rules ;
But hath thy mother brought a damsel home,
And let her see thy face, then all is one
As ye were wed."   He answered, " Even so,
It matters nothing ; therefore hear me, sir :
The damsel being mine, I am content
To let her do according to her will ;
And when we shall return, so surely, sir,
As I shall find her by my mother's side,
Then will I take her "; and he left to speak ;
His father answering, " Son, thy words are good."

BOOK VI.

NIGHT. Now a tent was pitched, and Japhet sat
      In the door and watched, for on a litter lay
The father of his love.   And he was sick
To death ; but daily he would rouse him up,
And stare upon the light, and ever say,
" On, let us journey " ; but it came to pass
That night, across their path a river ran,
And they who served the father and the son
Had pitched the tents beside it, and had made
A fire, to scare away the savagery
That roamed in that great forest, for their way
Had led among the trees of God.

                              The moon
Shone on the river, like a silver road
To lead them over ; but when Japhet looked,
He said, " We shall not cross it.   I shall lay
This well-belovéd head low in the leaves, —
Not on the farther side."   From time to time,
The water-snakes would stir its glassy flow
With curling undulations, and would lay
Their heads along the bank, and, subtle-eyed,
Consider those long spirting flames, that danced,
When some red log would break and crumble down,
And show his dark despondent eyes, that watched,
Wearily, even Japhet's.   But he cared

Little ; and in the dark, that was not dark,
But dimness of confused incertitude,
Would move a-near all silently, and gaze
And breathe, and shape itself, a maned thing
With eyes ; and still he cared not, and the form
Would falter, then recede, and melt again
Into the farther shade.   And Japhet said :
" How long ?   The moon hath grown again in heaven,
After her caving twice, since we did leave
The threshold of our home ; and now what 'vails
That far on tumbled mountain snow we toiled,
Hungry, and weary, all the day ; by night
Waked with a dreadful trembling underneath,
To look, while every cone smoked, and there ran
Red brooks adown, that licked the forest up,
While in the pale white ashes wading on
We saw no stars ? — what 'vails if afterward,
Astonished with great silence, we did move
Over the measureless, unknown desert mead ;
While all the day, in rents and crevices,
Would lie the lizard and the serpent kind,
Drowsy ; and in the night take fearsome shapes,
And oft-times woman-faced and woman-haired
Would trail their snaky length, and curse and mourn ;
Or there would wander up, when we were tired,
Dark troops of evil ones, with eyes morose,
Withstanding us, and staring ; — O ! what 'vails
That in the dread deep forest we have fought
With following packs of wolves ?   These men of might,

Even the giants, shall not hear the doom
My father came to tell them of. Ah, me !
If God indeed had sent him, would he lie
(For he is stricken with a sore disease)
Helpless outside their city ? "

                            Then he rose,
And put aside the curtains of the tent,
To look upon his father's face ; and lo !
The tent being dark, he thought that somewhat sat
Beside the litter ; and he set his eyes
To see it, and saw not ; but only marked
Where, fallen away from manhood and from power,
His father lay. Then he came forth again,
Trembling, and crouched beside the dull red fire,
And murmured, " Now it is the second time :
An old man, as I think (but scarcely saw),
Dreadful of might. Its hair was white as wool :
I dared not look ; perhaps I saw not aught,
But only knew that it was there : the same
Which walked beside us once when he did pray."
And Japhet hid his face between his hands
For fear, and grief of heart, and weariness
Of watching ; and he slumbered not, but mourned
To himself, a little moment, as it seemed,
For sake of his loved father : then he lift
His eyes, and day had dawned. Right suddenly
The moon withheld her silver, and she hung
Frail as a cloud. The ruddy flame that played,
By night on dim, dusk trees, and on the flood,

Crept red amongst the logs, and all the world
And all the water blushed and bloomed. The stars
Were gone, and golden shafts came up, and touched
The feathered heads of palms, and green was born
Under the rosy cloud, and purples flew
Like veils across the mountains ; and he saw,
Winding athwart them, bathed in blissful peace,
And the sacredness of morn, the battlements
And out-posts of the giants ; and there ran
On the other side the river, as it were,
White mounds of marble, tabernacles fair,
And towers below a line of inland cliff :
These were their fastnesses, and here their homes.

In valleys and the forest, all that night,
There had been woe ; in every hollow place,
And under walls, like drifted flowers, or snow,
Women lay mourning ; for the serpent lodged
That night within the gates, and had decreed,
" I will (or ever I come) that ye drive out
The women, the abhorréd of my soul."
Therefore, more beauteous than all climbing bloom,
Purple and scarlet, cumbering of the boughs,
Or flights of azure doves that lit to drink
The water of the river ; or, new born,
The quivering butterflies in companies,
That slowly crept adown the sandy marge,
Like living crocus beds, and also drank,
And rose an orange cloud ; their hollowed hands

They dipped between the lilies, or with robes
Full of ripe fruitage, sat and peeled and ate,
Weeping ; or comforting their little ones,
And lulling them with sorrowful long hymns
Among the palms.

        So went the earlier morn.
Then came a messenger, while Japhet sat
Mournfully, and he said, ' The men of might
Are willing ; let thy master, youth, appear."
And Japhet said, " So be it " ; and he thought,
" Now will I trust in God " ; and he went in
And stood before his father, and he said,
" My father " ; but the Master answered not,
But gazed upon the curtains of his tent,
Nor knew that one had called him.   He was clad
As ready for the journey, and his feet
Were sandalled, and his staff was at his side ;
And Japhet took the gown of sacrifice
And spread it on him, and he laid his crown
Upon his knees, and he went forth, and lift
His hand to heaven, and cried, " My father's God ! "
But neither whisper came nor echo fell
When he did listen.   Therefore he went on :
" Behold, I have a thing to say to thee.
My father charged thy servant, ' Let not ruth
Prevail with thee, to turn and bear me hence,
For God appointed me my task, to preach
Before the mighty.'   I must do my part
(O ! let it not displease thee), for he said

But yesternight, 'When they shall send for me,
Take me before them.' And I sware to him.
I pray thee, therefore, count his life and mine
Precious; for I that sware, I will perform."

Then cried he to his people, " Let us hence :
Take up the litter." And they set their feet
Toward the raft whereby men crossed that flood.

And while they journeyed, lo, the giants sat
Within the fairest hall where all were fair,
Each on his carven throne, o'er-canopied
With work of women. And the dragon lay
In a place of honor ; and with subtlety
He counselled them, for they did speak by turns ;
And they being proud, might nothing master them,
But guile alone : and he did fawn on them ;
And when the younger taunted him, submiss
He testified great humbleness, and cried,
" A cruel God, forsooth ! but nay, O nay,
I will not think it of Him, that He meant
To threaten these. O, when I look on them,
How doth my soul admire."
                            And one stood forth,
The youngest ; of his brethren, named " the Rock."
" Speak out," quoth he, " thou toothless slavering thing,
What is it ? thinkest thou that such as we
Should be afraid ? What is this goodly doom ? "
And Satan laughed upon him. " Lo," said he,

8

" Thou art not fully grown, and every one
I look on, standeth higher by the head,
Yea, and the shoulders, than do other men ;
Forsooth, thy servant thought not thou wouldst fear,
Thou and thy fellows." Then with one accord,
" Speak," cried they ; and with mild persuasive eyes,
And flattering tongue, he spoke.

      " Ye mighty ones,
It hath been known to you these many days
How that for piety I am much famed.
I am exceeding pious : if I lie,
As hath been whispered, it is but for sake
Of God, and that ye should not think Him hard,
For I am all for God. Now some have thought
That He hath also (and it may be so
Or yet may not be so) on me been hard ;
Be not ye therefore wroth, for my poor sake ;
I am contented to have earned your weal,
Though I must therefore suffer.

       " Now to-day
One cometh, yea, an harmless man, a fool,
Who boasts he hath a message from our God,
And lest that you, for bravery of heart
And stoutness, being angered with his prate,
Should lift a hand, and kill him, I am here."

Then spoke the Leader, " How now, snake ? Thy words
Ring false. Why ever liest thou, snake, to us ?
Thou coward ! none of us will see thee harmed.

I say thou liest.   The land is strewed with slain ;
Myself have hewn down companies, and blood
Makes fertile all the field.   Thou knowest it well ;
And hast thou, driveller, panting sore for age,
Come with a force to bid us spare one fool ? "

And Satan answered, " Nay you ! be not wroth ;
Yet true it is, and yet not all the truth.
Your servant would have told the rest, if now
(For fulness of your life being fretted sore
At mine infirmities, which God in vain
I supplicate to heal) ye had not caused
My speech to stop."   And he they called " the Oak "
Made answer, " 'T is a good snake ; let him be.
Why would ye fright the poor old craven beast ?
Look how his lolling tongue doth foam for fear.
Ye should have mercy, brethren, on the weak.
Speak, dragon, thou hast leave ; make stout thy heart.
What ! hast thou lied to this great company ?
It was, we know it was, for humbleness ;
Thou wert not willing to offend with truth."

" Yea, majesties," quoth Satan, " thus it was,"
And lifted up appealing eyes, and groaned ;
" O, can it be, compassionate as brave,
And housed in cunning works themselves have reared,
And served in gold, and warmed with minivere,
And ruling nobly, — that He, not content
Unless alone He reigneth, looks to bend

Or break them in, like slaves to cry to Him,
' What is Thy will with us, O Master dear ? '
Or else to eat of death ?

         " For my part, lords,
I cannot think it : for my piety
And reason, which I also share with you,
Are my best lights, and ever counsel me,
' Believe not aught against thy God ; believe,
Since thou canst never reach to do Him wrong,
That He will never stoop to do thee wrong.
Is He not just and equal, yea, and kind ? '
Therefore, O majesties, it is my mind
Concerning him ye wot of, thus to think
The message is not like what I have learned
By reason and experience, of the God.
Therefore no message 't is.   The man is mad."
Thereat the great Leader laughed for scorn.   " Hold,
      snake ;
If God be just, there SHALL be reckoning days.
We rather would He were a partial God,
And being strong, He sided with the strong.
Turn now thy reason to the other side,
And speak for that ; for as to justice, snake,
We would have none of it."

         And Satan fawned :
" My lord is pleased to mock at my poor wit ;
Yet in my pious fashion I must talk :
For say that God was wroth with man, and came
And slew him, that should make an empty world,
But not a better nation."

This replied,
" Truth, dragon, yet He is not bound to mean
A better nation ; may be, He designs,
If none will turn again, a punishment
Upon an evil one."
                    And Satan cried,
" Alas ! my heart being full of love for men,
I cannot choose but think of God as like
To me ; and yet my piety concludes,
Since He will have your fear, that love alone
Sufficeth not, and I admire, and say,
' Give me, O friends, your love, and give to God
Your fear.' "   But they cried out in wrath and rage,
" We are not strong that any we will fear,
Nor specially a foe that means us ill."

BOOK VII.

AND while he spoke there was a noise without;
    The curtains of the door were flung aside,
And some with heavy feet bare in, and set
A litter on the floor.
            The Master lay
Upon it, but his eyes were dimmed and set;
And Japhet, in despairing weariness,
Leaned it beside. He marked the mighty ones,
Silent for pride of heart, and in his place
The jewelled dragon; and the dragon laughed,
And subtly peered at him, till Japhet shook
With rage and fear. The snaky wonder cried,
Hissing, " Thou brown-haired youth, come up to me;
I fain would have thee for my shrine afar,
To serve among an host as beautiful
As thou: draw near." It hissed, and Japhet felt
Horrible drawings, and cried out in fear,
" Father! O help, the serpent draweth me!"
And struggled and grew faint, as in the toils
A netted bird. But still his father lay
Unconscious, and the mighty did not speak,
But half in fear and half for wonderment
Beheld. And yet again the dragon laughed,
And leered at him and hissed; and Japhet strove
Vainly to take away his spell-set eyes,

And moved to go to him, till piercingly
Crying out, " God! forbid it, God in heaven !"
The dragon lowered his head, and shut his eyes
As feigning sleep ; and, suddenly released,
He fell back staggering ; and at noise of it,
And clash of Japhet's weapons on the floor,
And Japhet's voice crying out, "I loathe thee, snake !
I hate thee ! O, I hate thee !" came again,
The senses of the shipwright ; and he, moved,
And looking, as one 'mazed, distressfully
Upon the mighty, said, " One called on God :
Where is my God ?   If God have need of me,
Let Him come down and touch my lips with strength,
Or dying I shall die."
                              It came to pass,
While he was speaking, that the curtains swayed ;
A rushing wind did move throughout the place,
And all the pillars shook, and on the head
Of Noah the hair was lifted, and there played
A somewhat, as it were a light, upon
His breast ; then fell a darkness, and men heard
A whisper as of one that spake.   With that,
The daunted mighty ones kept silent watch
Until the wind had ceased and darkness fled.
When it grew light, there curled a cloud of smoke
From many censers where the dragon lay.
It hid him.   He had called his ministrants,
And bid them veil him thus, that none might look ;
Also the folk who came with Noah had fled.

But Noah was seen, for he stood up erect,
And leaned on Japhet's hand. Then, after pause,
The Leader said, " My brethren, it were well
(For naught we fear) to let this sorcerer speak."
And they did reach toward the man their staves,
And cry with loud accord, " Hail, sorcerer, hail ! "

And he made answer, " Hail ! I am a man
That is a shipwright. I was born afar
To Lamech, him that reigns a king, to wit,
Over the land of Jalal. Majesties,
I bring a message, — lay you it to heart ;
For there is wrath in heaven : my God is wroth.
' Prepare your houses, or I come,' saith He,
' A Judge.' Now, therefore, say not in your hearts,
' What have we done ? ' Your dogs may answer that,
To make whom fiercer for the chase, ye feed
With captives whom ye slew not in the war,
But saved alive, and living throw to them
Daily. Your wives may answer that, whose babes
Their firstborn ye do take and offer up
To this abhorréd snake, while yet the milk
Is in their innocent mouths, — your maiden babes
Tender. Your slaves may answer that, — the gangs
Whose eyes ye did put out to make them work
By night unwitting (yea, by multitudes
They work upon the wheel in chains). Your friends
May answer that, — (their bleachéd bones cry out,)
For ye did, wickedly, to eat their lands,

Turn on their valleys, in a time of peace,
The rivers, and they, choking in the night,
Died unavenged. But rather (for I leave
To tell of more, the time would be so long
To do it, and your time, O mighty ones,
Is short), — but rather say, 'We sinners know
Why the Judge standeth at the door,' and turn
While yet there may be respite, and repent.

" ' Or else,' saith He that formed you, ' I swear,
By all the silence of the times to come,
By the solemnities of death, — yea, more,
By Mine own power and love which ye have scorned,
That I will come. I will command the clouds,
And raining they shall rain ; yea, I will stir
With all my storms the ocean for your sake,
And break for you the boundary of the deep.

" ' Then shall the mighty mourn.
                              Should I forbear,
That have been patient ? I will not forbear !
For yet,' saith He, ' the weak cry out ; for yet
The little ones do languish ; and the slave
Lifts up to Me his chain. I therefore, I
Will hear them. I by death will scatter you ;
Yea, and by death will draw them to My breast,
And gather them to peace.
                              " ' But yet,' saith He,
' Repent, and turn you. Wherefore will ye die ? '

8 *   L

" Turn then, O turn, while yet the enemy
Untamed of man fatefully moans afar ;
For if ye will not turn, the doom is near.
Then shall the crested wave make sport, and beat
You mighty at your doors.   Will ye be wroth?
Will ye forbid it?   Monsters of the deep
Shall suckle in your palaces their young,
And swim atween your hangings, all of them
Costly with broidered work, and rare with gold
And white and scarlet (there did ye oppress, —
There did ye make you vile) ; but ye shall lie
Meekly, and storm and wind shall rage above,
And urge the weltering wave.

      " ' Yet,' saith thy God,
' Son,' ay, to each of you He saith, ' O son,
Made in My image, beautiful and strong,
Why wilt thou die?   Thy Father loves thee well.
Repent and turn thee from thine evil ways,
O son ! and no more dare the wrath of love.
Live for thy Father's sake that forméd thee.
Why wilt thou die? '   Here will I make an end."

Now ever on his daïs the dragon lay,
Feigning to sleep ; and all the mighty ones
Were wroth, and chided, some against the woe,
And some at whom the sorcerer they had named, —
Some at their fellows, for the younger sort, —
As men the less acquaint with deeds of blood,
And given to learning and the arts of peace

(Their fathers having crushed rebellion out
Before their time) — lent favorable ears.
They said, " A man, or false or fanatic,
May claim good audience if he fill our ears
With what is strange : and we would hear again."

The Leader said, " An audience hath been given.
The man hath spoken, and his words are naught ;
A feeble threatener, with a foolish threat,
And it is not our manner that we sit
Beyond the noonday"; then they grandly rose,
A stalwart crowd, and with their Leader moved
To the tones of harping, and the beat of shawms,
And the noise of pipes, away.   But some were left
About the Master ; and the feigning snake
Couched on his daïs.
                         Then one to Japhet said,
One called " the Cedar-Tree," " Dost thou, too, think
To reign upon our lands when we lie drowned ?"
And Japhet said, " I think not, nor desire,
Nor in my heart consent, but that ye swear
Allegiance to the God, and live."   He cried,
To one surnamed " the Pine," — " Brother, behooves
That deep we cut our names in yonder crag,
Else when this youth returns, his sons may ask
Our names, and he may answer, ' Matters not,
For my part I forget them.' "
                         Japhet said,
" They might do worse than that, they might deny

That such as you have ever been."   With that
They answered, "No, thou dost not think it, no !"
And Japhet, being chafed, replied in heat,
"And wherefore ? if ye say of what is sworn,
'He will not do it,' shall it be more hard
For future men, if any talk on it,
To say, 'He did not do it' ?"   They replied,
With laughter, "Lo you! he is stout with us.
And yet he cowered before the poor old snake.
Sirrah, when you are saved, we pray you now
To bear our might in mind, — do, sirrah, do;
And likewise tell your sons, '"The Cedar Tree"
Was a good giant, for he struck me not,
Though he was young and full of sport, and though
I taunted him.' "

      With that they also passed.
But there remained who with the shipwright spoke :
"How wilt thou certify to us thy truth ?'
And he related to them all his ways
From the beginning : of the Voice that called ;
Moreover, how the ship of doom was built.

And one made answer, "Shall the mighty God
Talk with a man of wooden beams and bars ?
No, thou mad preacher, no.   If He, Eterne,
Be ordering of His far infinitudes,
And darkness cloud a world, it is but chance,
As if the shadow of His hand had fallen
On one that He forgot, and troubled it."

Then said the Master, "Yet, — who told thee so?"

And from his daïs the feigning serpent hissed:
"Preacher, the light within, it was that shined,
And told him so.   The pious will have dread
Him to declare such as ye rashly told.
The course of God is one.   It likes not us
To think of Him as being acquaint with change:
It were beneath Him.   Nay, the finished earth
Is left to her great masters.   They must rule;
They do; and I have set myself between, —
A visible thing for worship, sith His face
(For He is hard) He showeth not to men.
Yea, I have set myself 'twixt God and man,
To be interpreter, and teach mankind
A pious lesson by my piety,
He loveth not, nor hateth, nor desires, —
It were beneath Him."
     And the Master said,
"Thou liest.   Thou wouldst lie away the world,
If He, whom thou hast dared speak against,
Would suffer it."   "I may not chide with thee,"
It answered, "NOW; but if there come such time
As thou hast prophesied, as I now reign
In all men's sight, shall my dominion then
Reach to be mighty in their souls.   Thou too
Shalt feel it, prophet."   And he lowered his head.

Then quoth the Leader of the young men: "Sir,

We scorn you not ; speak further ; yet our thought
. First answer.   Not but by a miracle
Can this thing be.   The fashion of the world
We heretofore have never known to change ;
And will God change it now ? "

He then replied :
" What is thy thought ?   THERE IS NO MIRACLE ?
There is a great one, which thou hast not read,
And never shalt escape.   Thyself, O man,
Thou art the miracle.   Lo, if thou sayest,
' I am one, and fashioned like the gracious world,
Red clay is all my make, myself, my whole,
And not my habitation,' then thy sleep
Shall give thee wings to play among the rays
O' the morning.   If thy thought be, ' I am one, —
A spirit among spirits, — and the world
A dream my spirit dreameth of, my dream
Being all,' the dominating mountains strong
Shall not for that forbear to take thy breath,
And rage with all their winds, and beat thee back,
And beat thee down when thou wouldst set thy feet
Upon their awful crests.   Ay, thou thyself,
Being in the world and of the world, thyself
Hast breathed in breath from Him that made the world.
Thou dost inherit, as thy Maker's son,
That which He is, and that which He hath made :
Thou art thy Father's copy of Himself, —
THOU art thy FATHER'S MIRACLE.

Behold
He buildeth up the stars in companies ;

He made for them a law.   To man He said,
' Freely I give thee freedom.'   What remains?
O, it remains, if thou, the image of God,
Wilt reason well, that thou shalt know His ways;
But first thou must be loyal, — love, O man,
Thy Father, — hearken when He pleads with thee,
For there is something left of Him e'en now, —
A witness for thy Father in thy soul,
Albeit thy better state thou hast foregone.

" Now, then, be still, and think not in thy soul,
' The rivers in their course forever run,
And turn not from it.   He is like to them
Who made them.'   Think the rather, ' With my foot
I have turned the rivers from their ancient way,
To water grasses that were fading.   What!
Is God my Father as the river wave,
That yet descendeth, like the lesser thing
He made, and not like me, a living son,
That changed the watercourse to suit his will?'

" Man is the miracle in nature.   God
Is the ONE MIRACLE to man.   Behold,
' There is a God,' thou sayest.   Thou sayest well:
In that thou sayest all.   To Be is more
Of wonderful, than being, to have wrought,
Or reigned, or rested.
      Hold then there, content;
Learn that to love is the one way to know,

Or God or man : it is not love received
That maketh man to know the inner life
Of them that love him ; his own love bestowed
Shall do it.   Love thy Father, and no more
His doings shall be strange.   Thou shalt not fret
At any counsel, then, that He will send, —
No, nor rebel, albeit He have with thee
Great reservations.   Know, to Be is more
Than to have acted ; yea, or after rest
And patience, to have risen and been wroth,
Broken the sequence of an ordered earth,
And troubled nations."

                  Then the dragon sighed.
" Poor fanatic," quoth he, " thou speakest well.
Would I were like thee, for thy faith is strong,
Albeit thy senses wander.   Yea, good sooth,
My masters, let us not despise, but learn
Fresh loyalty from this poor loyal soul.
Let us go forth — (myself will also go
To head you) — and do sacrifice ; for that,
We know, is pleasing to the mighty God :
But as for building many arks of wood,
O majesties ! when He shall counsel you
HIMSELF, then build.   What say you, shall it be
An hundred oxen, — fat, well liking, white ?
An hundred ? why, a thousand were not much
To such as you."   Then Noah lift up his arms
To heaven, and cried, " Thou aged shape of sin,
The Lord rebuke thee."

BOOK VIII.

THEN one ran, crying, while Niloiya wrought,
   "The Master cometh!" and she went within
To adorn herself for meeting him. And Shem
Went forth and talked with Japhet in the field,
And said, "Is it well, my brother?" He replied,
" Well! and, I pray you, is it well at home?"

But Shem made answer, " Can a house be well,
If he that should command it bides afar?
Yet well is thee, because a fair free maid
Is found to wed thee; and they bring her in
This day at sundown. Therefore is much haste
To cover thick with costly webs the floor,
And pluck and cover thick the same with leaves
Of all sweet herbs, — I warrant, ye shall hear
No footfall where she treadeth ; and the seats
Are ready, spread with robes ; the tables set
With golden baskets, red pomegranates shred
To fill them ; and the rubied censers smoke,
Heaped up with ambergris and cinnamon,
And frankincense and cedar."
                  Japhet said,
" I will betroth her to me straight "; and went
(Yet labored he with sore disquietude)
To gather grapes, and reap and bind the sheaf

For his betrothal.   And his brother spake,
" Where is our father ? doth he preach to-day ? "
And Japhet answered, " Yea.   He said to me,
' Go forward ; I will follow when the folk
By yonder mountain-hold I shall have warned.' "

And Shem replied, " How thinkest thou ? — thine ears
Have heard him oft."   He answered, " I do think
These be the last days of this old fair world."

Then he did tell him of the giant folk :
How they, than he, were taller by the head ;
How one must stride that will ascend the steps
That lead to their wide halls ; and how they drave,
With manful shouts, the mammoth to the north ;
And how the talking dragon lied and fawned,
They seated proudly on their ivory thrones,
And scorning him : and of their peakéd hoods,
And garments wrought upon, each with the tale
Of him that wore it, — all his manful deeds
(Yea, and about their skirts were effigies
Of kings that they had slain ; and some, whose swords
Many had pierced, wore vestures all of red,
To signify much blood) : and of their pride
He told, but of the vision in the tent
He told him not.
                    And when they reached the house,
Niloiya met them, and to Japhet cried,
" All hail, right fortunate !   Lo, I have found

A maid. And now thou hast done well to reap
The late ripe corn." So he went in with her,
And she did talk with him right motherly :
" It hath been fully told me how ye loathed
To wed thy father's slave ; yea, she herself,
Did she not all declare to me ? "

He said,

" Yet is thy damsel fair, and wise of heart."
" Yea," quoth his mother ; " she made clear to me
How ye did weep, my son, and ye did vow,
' I will not take her !' Now it was not I
That wrought to have it so." And he replied,
" I know it." Quoth the mother, " It is well ;
For that same cause is laughter in my heart."
" But she is sweet of language," Japhet said.
" Ay," quoth Niloiya, " and thy wife no less
Whom thou shalt wed anon, — forsooth, anon, —
It is a lucky hour. Thou wilt ? " He said,
" I will." And Japhet laid the slender sheaf
From off his shoulder, and he said, " Behold,
My father ! " Then Niloiya turned herself,
And lo ! the shipwright stood. " All hail ! " quoth she.
And bowed herself, and kissed him on the mouth ;
But while she spake with him, sorely he sighed ;
And she did hang about his neck the robe
Of feasting, and she poured upon his hands
Clear water, and anointed him, and set
Before him bread.

And Japhet said to him,

"My father, my belovéd, wilt thou yet
Be sad because of scorning?   Eat this day;
For as an angel in their eyes thou art
Who stand before thee."   But he answered, "Peace!
Thy words are wide."
     And when Niloiya heard,
She said, "Is this a time for mirth of heart
And wine?   Behold, I thought to wed my son,
Even this Japhet; but is this a time,
When sad is he to whom is my desire,
And lying under sorrow as from God?"

He answered, "Yea, it is a time of times;
Bring in the maid."   Niloiya said, "The maid
That first I spoke on, shall not Japhet wed;
It likes not her, nor yet it likes not me.
But I have found another; yea, good sooth,
The damsel will not tarry, she will come
With all her slaves by sundown."
      And she said,
"Comfort thy heart, and eat: moreover, know
How that thy great work even to-day is done.
Sir, thy great ship is finished, and the folk
(For I, according to thy will, have paid
All that was left us to them for their wage,)
Have brought, as to a storehouse, flour of wheat,
Honey and oil, — much victual; yea, and fruits,
Curtains and household gear.   And, sir, they say
It is thy will to take it for thy hold

Our fastness and abode." He answeréd, "Yea,
Else wherefore was it built?" She said, "Good sir,
I pray you make us not the whole earth's scorn.
And now, to-morrow in thy father's house
Is a great feast, and weddings are toward;
Let be the ship, till after, for thy words
Have ever been, 'If God shall send a flood,
There will I dwell'; I pray you therefore wait
At least till He DOTH send it."

                      And he turned,
And answered nothing. Now the sun was low
While yet she spake; and Japhet came to them
In goodly raiment, and upon his arm
The garment of betrothal. And with that
A noise, and then brake in a woman slave
And Amarant. This, with folding of her hands,
Did say full meekly, "If I do offend,
Yet have not I been willing to offend;
For now this woman will not be denied
Herself to tell her errand."

                      And they sat.
Then spoke the woman, "If I do offend,
Pray you forgive the bondslave, for her tongue
Is for her mistress. 'Lo!' my mistress saith,
'Put off thy bravery, bridegroom; fold away,
Mother, thy webs of pride, thy costly robes
Woven of many colors. We have heard
Thy master. Lo, to-day right evil things
He prophesied to us, that were his friends;

Therefore, my answer : — God do so to me ;
Yea, God do so to me, more also, more
Than He did threaten, if my damsel's foot
Ever draw nigh thy door.' "

                 And when she heard,
Niloiya sat amazed, in grief of soul.
But Japhet came unto the slave, where low
She bowed herself for fear.   He said, " Depart ;
Say to thy mistress, ' It is well.' "   With that
She turned herself, and she made haste to flee,
Lest any, for those evil words she brought,
Would smite her.   But the bondmaid of the house
Lift up her hand and said, " If I offend,
It was not of my heart : thy damsel knew
Naught of this matter."   And he held to her
His hand and touched her, and said, " Amarant !"
And when she looked upon him, she did take
And spread before her face her radiant locks,
Trembling.   And Japhet said, " Lift up thy face,
O fairest of the daughters, thy fair face ;
For, lo ! the bridegroom standeth with the robe
Of thy betrothal !" — and he took her locks
In his two hands to part them from her brow,
And laid them on her shoulders ; and he said,
" Sweet are the blushes of thy face," and put
The robe upon her, having said, " Behold,
I have repented me ; and oft by night,
In the waste wilderness, while all things slept,
I thought upon thy words, for they were sweet.

" For this I make thee free.   And now thyself
Art loveliest in mine eyes ; I look, and lo !
Thou art of beauty more than any thought
I had concerning thee.   Let, then, this robe,
Wrought on with imagery of fruitful bough,
And graceful leaf, and birds with tender eyes,
Cover the ripples of thy tawny hair."
So when she held her peace, he brought her nigh
To hear the speech of wedlock ; ay, he took
The golden cup of wine to drink with her,
And laid the sheaf upon her arms.   He said,
" Like as my fathers in the older days
Led home the daughters whom they chose, do I ;
Like as they said, ' Mine honor have I set
Upon thy head !' do I.   Eat of my bread,
Rule in my house, be mistress of my slaves,
And mother of my children."

      And he brought
The damsel to his father, saying, " Behold
My wife !   I have betrothed her to myself ;
I pray you, kiss her."   And the Master did :
He said, " Be mother of a multitude,
And let them to their father even so
Be found, as he is found to me."

        With that
She answered, " Let this woman, sir, find grace
And favor in your sight."

       And Japhet said,
" Sweet mother, I have wed the maid ye chose

And brought me first.   I leave her in thy hand ;
Have care on her, till I shall come again
And ask her of thee."   So they went apart,
He and his father to the marriage feast.

BOOK IX.

THE prayer of Noah. The man went forth by night
        And listened; and the earth was dark and still,
And he was driven of his great distress
Into the forest; but the birds of night
Sang sweetly; and he fell upon his face,
And cried, " God, God! Thy billows and Thy waves
Have swallowed up my soul.

                            " Where is my God?
For I have somewhat yet to plead with Thee;
For I have walked the strands of Thy great deep,
Heard the dull thunder of its rage afar,
And its dread moaning. O, the field is sweet, —
Spare it. The delicate woods make white their trees
With blossom, — spare them. Life is sweet; behold
There is much cattle, and the wild and tame,
Father, do feed in quiet, — spare them.

                                    " God!
Where is my God? The long wave doth not rear
Her ghostly crest to lick the forest up,
And like a chief in battle fall, — not yet.
The lightnings pour not down, from ragged holes
In heaven, the torment of their forkéd tongues,
And, like fell serpents, dart and sting, — not yet.
The winds awake not, with their awful wings
To winnow, even as chaff, from out their track,

All that withstandeth, and bring down the pride
Of all things strong and all things high —

                             "Not yet.

O, let it not be yet.   Where is my God?
How am I saved, if I and mine be saved
Alone?   I am not saved, for I have loved
My country and my kin.   Must I, Thy thrall,
Over their lands be lord when they are gone?
I would not: spare them, Mighty.   Spare Thyself,
For Thou dost love them greatly, — and if not . . . ."

Another praying unremote, a Voice
Calm as the solitude between wide stars.

"Where is my God, who loveth this lost world, —
Lost from its place and name, but won for Thee?
Where is my multitude, my multitude,
That I shall gather?"   And white smoke went up
From incense that was burning, but there gleamed
No light of fire, save dimly to reveal
The whiteness rising, as the prayer of him
That mourned.   "My God, appear for me, appear;
Give me my multitude, for it is mine.
The bitterness of death I have not feared,
To-morrow shall Thy courts, O God, be full.
Then shall the captive from his bonds go free,
Then shall the thrall find rest, that knew not rest
From labor and from blows.   The sorrowful —
That said of joy, 'What is it?' and of songs,

'We have not heard them ' — shall be glad and sing ;
Then shall the little ones that knew not Thee,
And such as heard not of Thee, see Thy face,
And seeing, dwell content."

The prayer of Noah.

He cried out in the darkness, " Hear, O God,
Hear Him : hear this one ; through the gates of death,
If life be all past praying for, O give
To Thy great multitude a way to peace ;
Give them to Him.

"But yet," said he, " O yet,
If there be respite for the terrible,
The proud, yea, such as scorn Thee, — and if not . . . .
Let not mine eyes behold their fall."

He cried,

" Forgive.   I have not done Thy work, Great Judge,
With a perfect heart; I have but half believed,
While in accustomed language I have warned ;
And now there is no more to do, no place
For my repentance, yea, no hour remains
For doing of that work again.   O, lost,
Lost world!"   And while he prayed, the daylight dawned.

And Noah went up into the ship, and sat
Before the Lord.   And all was still ; and now
In that great quietness the sun came up,
And there were marks across it, as it were

The shadow of a Hand upon the sun, —
Three fingers dark and dread, and afterward
There rose a white, thick mist, that peacefully
Folded the fair earth in her funeral shroud,
The earth that gave no token, save that now
There fell a little trembling under foot.

And Noah went down, and took and hid his face
Behind his mantle, saying, " I have made
Great preparation, and it may be yet,
Beside my house, whom I did charge to come
This day to meet me, there may enter in
Many that yesternight thought scorn of all
My bidding."   And because the fog was thick,
He said, " Forbid it, Heaven, if such there be,
That they should miss the way."   And even then
There was a noise of weeping and lament ;
The words of them that were affrighted, yea,
And cried for grief of heart.   There came to him
The mother and her children, and they cried,
" Speak, father, what is this?   What hast thou done? "
And when he lifted up his face, he saw
Japhet, his well-belovéd, where he stood
Apart ; and Amarant leaned upon his breast,
And hid her face, for she was sore afraid ;
And lo ! the robes of her betrothal gleamed
White in the deadly gloom.
                              And at his feet
The wives of his two other sons did kneel,
And wring their hands.

One cried, " O, speak to us ;
We are affrighted ; we have dreamed a dream,
Each to herself.   For me, I saw in mine
The grave old angels, like to shepherds, walk,
Much cattle following them.   Thy daughter looked,
And they did enter here."
                          The other lay
And moaned, " Alas ! O father, for my dream
Was evil : lo, I heard when it was dark,
I heard two wicked ones contend for me.
One said, ' And wherefore should this woman live,
When only for her children, and for her,
Is woe and degradation ? '   Then he laughed,
The other crying, ' Let alone, O prince ;
Hinder her not to live and bear much seed,
Because I hate her.' "
                          But he said, " Rise up,
Daughters of Noah, for I have learned no words
To comfort you."   Then spake her lord to her,
" Peace ! or I swear that for thy dream, myself
Will hate thee also."
              .   And Niloiya said,
" My sons, if one of you will hear my words,
Go now, look out, and tell me of the day,
How fares it ? "
                          And the fateful darkness grew.
But Shem went up to do his mother's will ;
And all was one as though the frighted earth
Quivered and fell a-trembling ; then they hid

Their faces every one, till he returned,
And spake not.   " Nay," they cried, " what hast thou
    seen ?
O, is it come to this ? "   He answered them,
" The door is shut."

CONTRASTED SONGS.

CONTRASTED SONGS.

—◆—

SAILING BEYOND SEAS.

(*Old Style.*)

METHOUGHT the stars were blinking bright,
    And the old brig's sails unfurled ;
    I said, " I will sail to my love this night
  At the other side of the world."
I stepped aboard, — we sailed so fast, —
  The sun shot up from the bourne ;
But a dove that perched upon the mast
  Did mourn, and mourn, and mourn.
      O fair dove ! O fond dove !
        And dove with the white breast,
     Let me alone, the dream is my own,
      And my heart is full of rest.

My true love fares on this great hill,
  Feeding his sheep for aye ;
I looked in his hut, but all was still,
  My love was gone away.

9*

I went to gaze in the forest creek,
  And the dove mourned on apace;
No flame did flash, nor fair blue reek
  Rose up to show me his place.
    O last love! O first love!
      My love with the true heart,
        To think I have come to this your home,
        And yet — we are apart!

My love! He stood at my right hand,
  His eyes were grave and sweet.
Methought he said, " In this far land,
  O, is it thus we meet!
Ah, maid most dear, I am not here;
  I have no place, — no part, —
No dwelling more by sea or shore,
  But only in thy heart."
    O fair dove! O fond dove!
      Till night rose over the bourne,
        The dove on the mast, as we sailed fast,
        Did mourn, and mourn, and mourn.

REMONSTRANCE.

DAUGHTERS of Eve! your mother did not well:
   She laid the apple in your father's hand,
And we have read, O wonder! what befell, —
   The man was not deceived, nor yet could stand:
He chose to lose, for love of her, his throne, —
With her could die, but could not live alone.

Daughters of Eve! he did not fall so low,
   Nor fall so far, as that sweet woman fell;
For something better, than as gods to know,
   That husband in that home left off to dwell:
For this, till love be reckoned less than lore,
Shall man be first and best for evermore.

Daughters of Eve! it was for your dear sake
   The world's first hero died an uncrowned king;
But God's great pity touched the grand mistake,
   And made his married love a sacred thing:
For yet his nobler sons, if aught be true,
Find the lost Eden in their love to you.

SONG FOR THE NIGHT OF CHRIST'S RESURRECTION.

(A Humble Imitation.)

" And birds of calm sit brooding on the charmèd wave."

IT is the noon of night,
And the world's Great Light
Gone out, she widow-like doth carry her:
The moon hath veiled her face,
Nor looks on that dread place
Where He lieth dead in scalèd sepulchre;
And heaven and hades, emptied, lend
Their flocking multitudes to watch and wait the end.

Tier above tier they rise,
Their wings now line the skies,
And shed out comforting light among the stars;
But they of the other place
The heavenly signs deface,
The gloomy brand of hell their brightness mars;
Yet high they sit in thronèd state, —
It is the hour of darkness to them dedicate.

And first and highest set,
Where the black shades are met,
The lord of night and hades leans him down;

His gleaming eyeballs show
More awful than the glow,
Which hangeth by the points of his dread crown;
And at his feet, where lightnings play,
The fatal sisters sit and weep, and curse their day.

Lo! one, with eyes all wide,
As she were sight denied,
Sits blindly feeling at her distaff old;
One, as distraught with woe,
Letting the spindle go,
Her star y-sprinkled gown doth shivering fold;
And one right mournful hangs her head,
Complaining, "Woe is me! I may not cut the thread.

"All men of every birth,
Yea, great ones of the earth,
Kings and their councillors, have I drawn down;
But I am held of Thee, —
Why dost Thou trouble me,
To bring me up, dead King, that keep'st Thy crown?
Yet for all courtiers hast but ten
Lowly, unlettered, Galilean fishermen.

"Olympian heights are bare
Of whom men worshipped there,
Immortal feet their snows may print no more;
Their stately powers below
Lie desolate, nor know

This thirty years Thessalian grove or shore;
　　But I am elder far than they; —
Where is the sentence writ that I must pass away?

　　" Art thou come up for this,
　　Dark regent, awful Dis?
And hast thou moved the deep to mark our ending?
　　And stirred the dens beneath,
　　To see us eat of death,
With all the scoffing heavens toward us bending?
　　Help! powers of ill, see not us die!"
But neither demon dares, nor angel deigns, reply.

　　Her sisters, fallen on sleep,
　　Fade in the upper deep,
And their grim lord sits on, in doleful trance;
　　Till her black veil she rends,
　　And with her death-shriek bends
Downward the terrors of her countenance;
　　Then, whelmed in night and no more seen,
They leave the world a doubt if ever such have been.

　　And the winged armies twain
　　Their awful watch maintain;
They mark the earth at rest with her Great Dead.
　　· Behold, from Antres wide,
　　Green Atlas heave his side;
His moving woods their scarlet clusters shed,
　　The swathing coif his front that cools,
And tawny lions lapping at his palm-edged pools.

Then like a heap of snow,
Lying where grasses grow,
See glimmering, while the moony lustres creep,
Mild mannered Athens, dight
In dewy marbles white,
Among her goddesses and gods asleep ;
And swaying on a purple sea,
The many moored galleys clustering at her quay.

Also, 'neath palm-trees' shade,
Amid their camels laid,
The pastoral tribes with all their flocks at rest ;
Like to those old-world folk,
With whom two angels broke
The bread of men at Abram's courteous 'quest,
When, listening as they prophesied,
His desert princess, being reproved, her laugh denied.

Or from the Morians' land
See worshipped Nilus bland,
Taking the silver road he gave the world,
To wet his ancient shrine
With waters held divine,
And touch his temple steps with wavelets curled,
And list, ere darkness change to gray,
Old minstrel-throated Memnon chanting in the day.

Moreover, Indian glades,
Where kneel the sun-swart maids,

On Gunga's flood their votive flowers to throw,
And launch i' the sultry night
Their burning cressets bright,
Most like a fleet of stars that southing go,
Till on her bosom prosperously
She floats them shining forth to sail the lulléd sea.

Nor bend they not their eyn
Where the watch-fires shine,
By shepherds fed, on hills of Bethlehem :
They mark, in goodly wise,
The city of David rise,
The gates and towers of rare Jerusalem ;
And hear the 'scapéd Kedron fret,
And night dews dropping from the leaves of Olivet.

But now the setting moon
To curtained lands must soon,
In her obedient fashion, minister ;
She first, as loath to go,
Lets her last silver flow
Upon her Master's sealéd sepulchre ;
And trees that in the gardens spread,
She kisseth all for sake of His low-lying head,

Then 'neath the rim goes down ;
And night with darker frown
Sinks on the fateful garden watchéd long ;
When some despairing eyes,

Far in the murky skies,
The unwishéd waking by their gloom foretell;
And blackness up the welkin swings,
And drinks the mild effulgence from celestial wings.

Last, with amazéd cry,
The hosts asunder fly,
Leaving an empty gulf of blackest hue;
Whence straightway shooteth down,
By the Great Father thrown,
A mighty angel, strong and dread to view;
And at his fall the rocks are rent,
The waiting world doth quake with mortal tremblement;

The regions far and near
Quail with a pause of fear,
More terrible than aught since time began;
The winds, that dare not fleet,
Drop at his awful feet,
And in its bed wails the wide ocean;
The flower of dawn forbears to blow,
And the oldest running river cannot skill to flow.

At stand, by that dread place,
He lifts his radiant face,
And looks to heaven with reverent love and fear;
Then, while the welkin quakes,
The muttering thunder breaks,
And lightnings shoot and ominous meteors drear,

And all the daunted earth doth moan,
He from the doors of death rolls back the sealéd stone. —

— In regal quiet deep,
Lo, One new waked from sleep!
Behold, He standeth in the rock-hewn door!
Thy children shall not die, —
Peace, peace, thy Lord is by!
He liveth! — they shall live for evermore.
Peace! lo, He lifts a priestly hand,
And blesseth all the sons of men in every land.

Then, with great dread and wail,
Fall down, like storms of hail,
The legions of the lost in fearful wise;
And they whose blissful race
Peoples the better place,
Lift up their wings to cover their fair eyes,
And through the waxing saffron brede,
Till they are lost in light, recede, and yet recede.

So while the fields are dim,
And the red sun his rim
First heaves, in token of his reign benign,
All stars the most admired,
Into their blue retired,
Lie hid, — the faded moon forgets to shine, —
And, hurrying down the sphery way,
Night flies, and sweeps her shadows from the paths of day.

But look! the Saviour blest,
Calm after solemn rest,
Stands in the garden 'neath His olive boughs;
The earliest smile of day
Doth on His vesture play,
And light the majesty of His still brows;
While angels hang with wings outspread,
Holding the new-won crown above His saintly head.

SONG OF MARGARET.

AY, I saw her, we have met, —
Married eyes how sweet they be, —
Are you happier, Margaret,
Than you might have been with me?
Silence! make no more ado!
Did she think I should forget?
Matters nothing, though I knew,
Margaret, Margaret.

Once those eyes, full sweet, full shy,
Told a certain thing to mine;
What they told me I put by,
O, so careless of the sign.
Such an easy thing to take,
And I did not want it then;

Fool ! I wish my heart would break,
   Scorn is hard on hearts of men.

Scorn of self is bitter work, —
   Each of us has felt it now :
Bluest skies she counted mirk,
   Self-betrayed of eyes and brow ;
As for me, I went my way,
   And a better man drew nigh,
Fain to earn, with long essay,
   What the winner's hand threw by.

Matters not in deserts old,
   What was born, and waxed, and yearned,
Year to year its meaning told,
   I am come, — its deeps are learned, —
Come, but there is naught to say, —
   Married eyes with mine have met.
Silence ! O, I had my day,
   Margaret, Margaret.

———

SONG OF THE GOING AWAY.

" OLD man, upon the green hillside,
   With yellow flowers besprinkled o'er,
How long in silence wilt thou bide
   At this low stone door?

" I stoop: within 't is dark and still ;
  But shadowy paths methinks there be,
And lead they far into the hill ? "
  " Traveller, come and see."

" 'T is dark, 't is cold, and hung with gloom ;
  I care not now within to stay ;
For thee and me is scarcely room,
  I will hence away."

" Not so, not so, thou youthful guest,
  Thy foot shall issue forth no more :
Behold the chamber of thy rest,
  And the closing door ! "

" O, have I 'scaped the whistling ball,
  And striven on smoky fields of fight,
And scaled the 'leaguered city's wall
  In the dangerous night ;

" And borne my life unharmèd still
  Through foaming gulfs of yeasty spray,
To yield it on a grassy hill
  At the noon of day ? "

" Peace ! Say thy prayers, and go to sleep,
  Till *some time*, One my seal shall break,
And deep shall answer unto deep,
  When He crieth, ' Awake ! ' "

A LILY AND A LUTE.

(Song of the uncommunicated Ideal.)

I.

I OPENED the eyes of my soul.
>   And behold,
A white river-lily : a lily awake, and aware, —
For she set her face upward, — aware how in scarlet and
>   gold
A long wrinkled cloud, left behind of the wandering air,
>   Lay over with fold upon fold,
>   With fold upon fold.

And the blushing sweet shame of the cloud made her
>   also ashamed,
The white river-lily, that suddenly knew she was fair ;
And over the far-away mountains that no man hath named,
>   And that no foot hath trod,
Flung down out of heavenly places, there fell, as it were,
A rose-bloom, a token of love, that should make them
>   endure,
Withdrawn in snow silence forever, who keep themselves
>   pure,
>   And look up to God.

Then I said, " In rosy air,
Cradled on thy reaches fair,
While the blushing early ray
Whitens into perfect day,
River-lily, sweetest known,
Art thou set for me alone ?
Nay, but I will bear thee far,
Where yon clustering steeples are,
And the bells ring out o'erhead,
And the stated prayers are said ;
And the busy farmers pace,
Trading in the market-place ;
And the country lasses sit,
By their butter, praising it ;
And the latest news is told,
While the fruit and cream are sold ;
And the friendly gossips greet,
Up and down the sunny street.
For," I said, " I have not met,
White one, any folk as yet
Who would send no blessing up,
Looking on a face like thine ;
For thou art as Joseph's cup,
And by thee might they divine.

" Nay ! but thou a spirit art ;
Men shall take thee in the mart
For the ghost of their best thought,
Raised at noon, and near them brought ;

Or the prayer they made last night,
Set before them all in white."

And I put out my rash hand,
For I thought to draw to land
The white lily.   Was it fit
Such a blossom should expand,
Fair enough for a world's wonder,
And no mortal gather it?
No.   I strove, and it went under,
And I drew, but it went down;
And the waterweeds' long tresses,
And the overlapping cresses,
Sullied its admired crown.
Then along the river strand,
Trailing, wrecked, it came to land,
Of its beauty half despoiled,
And its snowy pureness soiled:
O! I took it in my hand, —
You will never see it now,
White and golden as it grew:
No, I cannot show it you,
Nor the cheerful town endow
With the freshness of its brow.

If a royal painter, great
With the colors dedicate
To a dove's neck, a sea-bight,
And the flickerings over white

Mountain summits far away, —
One content to give his mind
To the enrichment of mankind,
And the laying up of light
In men's houses, — on that day,
Could have passed in kingly mood,
Would he ever have endued
Canvas with the peerless thing,
In the grace that it did bring,
And the light that o'er it flowed,
With the pureness that it showed,
And the pureness that it meant?
Could he skill to make it seen
As he saw?   For this, I ween,
He were likewise impotent.

II.

I opened the doors of my heart.

And behold,

There was music within and a song,
And echoes did feed on the sweetness, repeating it long.
I opened the doors of my heart: and behold,
There was music that played itself out in æolian notes;
Then was heard, as a far-away bell at long intervals tolled,

That murmurs and floats,

And presently dieth, forgotten of forest and wold,
And comes in all passion again, and a tremblement soft,

That maketh the listener full oft

To whisper, " Ah ! would I might hear it for ever and aye,
    When I toil in the heat of the day,
    When I walk in the cold."

I opened the door of my heart.   And behold,
  There was music within, and a song.
But while I was hearkening, lo, blackness without, thick
    and strong,
Came up and came over, and all that sweet fluting was
    drowned,
    I could hear it no more ;
For the welkin was moaning, the waters were stirred on
    the shore,
    And trees in the dark all around
Were shaken.   It thundered.   " Hark, hark ! there is
    thunder to-night !
The sullen long wave rears her head, and comes down
    with a will ;
The awful white tongues are let loose, and the stars are
    all dead ; —
There is thunder ! it thunders ! and ladders of light
    Run up.   There is thunder ! " I said,
" Loud thunder ! it thunders ! and up in the dark over-
    head,
A down-pouring cloud, (there is thunder !) a down-pour-
    ing cloud
Hails out her fierce message, and quivers the deep in
    its bed,
And cowers the earth held at bay ; and they mutter aloud,

And pause with an ominous tremble, till, great in their
    rage,
The heavens and earth come together, and meet with a
    crash ;
And the fight is so fell as if Time had come down with
    the flash,
    And the story of life was all read,
    And the Giver had turned the last page.

" Now their bar the pent water-floods lash,
And the forest trees give out their language austere with
    great age ;
    And there flieth o'er moor and o'er hill,
    And there heaveth at intervals wide,
The long sob of nature's great passion as loath to subside,
    Until quiet drop down on the tide,
    And mad Echo had moaned herself still."

    Lo ! or ever I was 'ware,
    In the silence of the air,
    Through my heart's wide-open door,
    Music floated forth once more,
    Floated to the world's dark rim,
    And looked over with a hymn ;
    Then came home with flutings fine,
    And discoursed in tones divine
    Of a certain grief of mine ;
    And went downward and went in,

Glimpses of my soul to win,
And discovered such a deep
That I could not choose but weep,
For it lay, a land-locked sea,
Fathomless and dim to me.

O, the song! it came and went,
    Went and came.
                I have not learned
Half the lore whereto it yearned,
Half the magic that it meant.
Water booming in a cave;
Or the swell of some long wave,
Setting in from unrevealed
Countries; or a foreign tongue,
Sweetly talked and deftly sung,
While the meaning is half sealed;
May be like it.   You have heard
Also; — can you find a word
For the naming of such song?
No; a name would do it wrong.
You have heard it in the night,
In the dropping rain's despite,
In the midnight darkness deep,
When the children were asleep,
And the wife, — no, let that be;
She asleep!   She knows right well
What the song to you and me,
While we breathe, can never tell;

She hath heard its faultless flow,
Where the roots of music grow.

While I listened, like young birds,
Hints were fluttering; almost words, —
Leaned and leaned, and nearer came ; —
Everything had changed its name.

Sorrow was a ship, I found,
Wrecked with them that in her are,
On an island richer far
Than the port where they were bound.
Fear was but the awful boom
Of the old great bell of doom,
Tolling, far from earthly air,
For all worlds to go to prayer.
Pain, that to us mortal clings,
But the pushing of our wings,
That we have no use for yet,
And the uprooting of our feet
From the soil where they are set,
And the land we reckon sweet.
Love in growth, the grand deceit
Whereby men the perfect greet ;
Love in wane, the blessing sent
To be (howsoe'er it went)
Never more with earth content.

O, full sweet, and O, full high,
Ran that music up the sky;
But I cannot sing it you,
More than I can make you view,
With my paintings labial,
Sitting up in awful row,
White old men majestical,
Mountains, in their gowns of snow,
Ghosts of kings; as my two eyes,
Looking over speckled skies,
See them now.   About their knees,
Half in haze, there stands at ease
A great army of green hills,
Some bareheaded; and, behold,
Small green mosses creep on some.
Those be mighty forests old;
And white avalanches come
Through yon rents, where now distils
Sheeny silver, pouring down
To a tune of old renown,
Cutting narrow pathways through
Gentian belts of airy blue,
To a zone where starwort blows,
And long reaches of the rose.

So, that haze all left behind,
Down the chestnut forests wind,
Past yon jagged spires, where yet

Foot of man was never set ;
Past a castle yawning wide,
With a great breach in its side,
To a nest-like valley, where,
Like a sparrow's egg in hue,
Lie two lakes, and teach the true
Color of the sea-maid's hair.

What beside ?   The world beside !
Drawing down and down, to greet
Cottage clusters at our feet, —
Every scent of summer tide, —
Flowery pastures all aglow
(Men and women mowing go
Up and down them) ; also soft
Floating of the film aloft,
Fluttering of the leaves alow.
Is this told?   It is not told.
Where's the danger? where's the cold
Slippery danger up the steep?
Where you shadow fallen asleep?
Chirping bird and tumbling spray,
Light, work, laughter, scent of hay,
Peace, and echo, where are they ?

Ah, they sleep, sleep all untold ;
Memory must their grace enfold

Silently ; and that high song
Of the heart, it doth belong
To the hearers.   Not a whit,
Though a chief musician heard,
Could he make a tune for it.

Though a lute full deftly strung,
And the sweetest bird e'er sung,
Could have tried it, — O, the lute
For that wondrous song were mute,
And the bird would do her part,
Falter, fail, and break her heart, —
Break her heart, and furl her wings,
On the unexpressive strings.

GLADYS AND HER ISLAND.

(On the Advantages of the Poetical Temperament.)

AN IMPERFECT FABLE WITH A DOUBTFUL MORAL.

HAPPY Gladys! I rejoice with her,
For Gladys saw the island.

It was thus:
They gave a day for pleasure in the school
Where Gladys taught; and all the other girls
Were taken out, to picnic in a wood.
But it was said, "We think it were not well
That little Gladys should acquire a taste
For pleasure, going about, and needless change.
It would not suit her station: discontent
Might come of it; and all her duties now
She does so pleasantly, that we were best
To keep her humble." So they said to her,
"Gladys, we shall not want you, all to-day.
Look, you are free; you need not sit at work:
No, you may take a long and pleasant walk
Over the sea-cliff, or upon the beach
Among the visitors."

Then Gladys blushed

10 *   O

For joy, and thanked them.   What! a holiday,
A whole one, for herself!   How good, how kind !
With that, the marshalled carriages drove off ;
And Gladys, sobered with her weight of joy,
Stole out beyond the groups upon the beach —
The children with their wooden spades, the band
That played for lovers, and the sunny stir
Of cheerful life and leisure — to the rocks,
For these she wanted most, and there was time
To mark them ; how like ruined organs prone
They lay, or leaned their giant fluted pipes,
And let the great white-crested reckless wave
Beat out their booming melody.

                       The sea
Was filled with light ; in clear blue caverns curled
The breakers, and they ran, and seemed to romp,
As playing at some rough and dangerous game,
While all the nearer waves rushed in to help,
And all the farther heaved their heads to peep,
And tossed the fishing boats.   Then Gladys laughed,
And said, " O, happy tide, to be so lost
In sunshine, that one dare not look at it ;
And lucky cliffs, to be so brown and warm ;
And yet how lucky are the shadows, too,
That lurk beneath their ledges.   It is strange,
That in remembrance though I lay them up,
They are forever, when I come to them,
Better than I had thought.   O, something yet
I had forgotten.   Oft I say, ' At least

This picture is imprinted; thus and thus,
The sharpened serried jags run up, run out,
Layer on layer.'   And I look — up — up —
High, higher up again, till far aloft
They cut into their ether, — brown, and clear,
And perfect.   And I, saying, 'This is mine,
To keep,' retire ; but shortly come again,
And they confound me with a glorious change.
The low sun out of rain-clouds stares at them ;
They redden, and their edges drip with — what ?
I know not, but 't is red.   It leaves no stain,
For the next morning they stand up like ghosts
In a sea-shroud and fifty thousand mews
Sit there, in long white files, and chatter on,
Like silly school-girls in their silliest mood.

"There is the boulder where we always turn.
O! I have longed to pass it ; now I will.
What would THEY say ? for one must slip and spring ;
'Young ladies! Gladys! I am shocked.   My dears,
Decorum, if you please : turn back at once.
Gladys, we blame you most ; you should have looked
Before you.'   Then they sigh, — how kind they are ! —
'What will become of you, if all your life
You look a long way off? — look anywhere,
And everywhere, instead of at your feet,
And where they carry you !'   Ah, well, I know
It is a pity," Gladys said ; " but then
We cannot all be wise: happy for me,

That other people are.
               "And yet I wish, —
For sometimes very right and serious thoughts
Come to me, — I do wish that they would come
When they are wanted! — when I teach the sums
On rainy days, and when the practising
I count to, and the din goes on and on,
Still the same tune and still the same mistake,
Then I am wise enough : sometimes I feel
Quite old.   I think that it will last, and say,
' Now my reflections do me credit ! now
I am a woman !' and I wish they knew
How serious all my duties look to me.
And how, my heart hushed down and shaded lies,
Just like the sea when low, convenient clouds,
Come over, and drink all its sparkles up.
But does it last ?   Perhaps, that very day,
The front door opens : out we walk in pairs ;
And I am so delighted with this world,
That suddenly has grown, being new washed,
To such a smiling, clean, and thankful world,
And with a tender face shining through tears,
Looks up into the sometime lowering sky,
That has been angry, but is reconciled,
And just forgiving her, that I, — that I, —
O, I forget myself : what matters how !
And then I hear (but always kindly said)
Some words that pain me so, — but just, but true :
' For if your place in this establishment

Be but subordinate, and if your birth
Be lowly, it the more behooves, — well, well,
No more.   We see that you are sorry.'   Yes!
I am always sorry THEN ; but now, — O, now,
Here is a bight more beautiful than all."

"And did they scold her, then, my pretty one?
And did she want to be as wise as they,
To bear a bucklered heart and priggish mind?
Ay, you may crow ; she did! but no, no, no,
The night-time will not let her, all the stars
Say nay to that, — the old sea laughs at her.
Why, Gladys is a child ; she has not skill
To shut herself within her own small cell,
And build the door up, and to say, ' Poor me !
I am a prisoner '; then to take hewn stones,
And, having built the windows up, to say,
' O, it is dark ! there is no sunshine here ;
There never has been.' "
                              Strange ! how very strange !
A woman passing Gladys with a babe,
To whom she spoke these words, and only looked
Upon the babe, who crowed and pulled her curls,
And never looked at Gladys, never once.
" A simple child," she added, and went by,
" To want to change her greater for their less ;
But Gladys shall not do it, no, not she ;
We love her — don't we ? — far too well for that."

Then Gladys, flushed with shame and keen surprise,
" How could she be so near, and I not know ?
And have I spoken out my thought aloud ?
I must have done, forgetting.   It is well
She walks so fast, for I am hungry now,
And here is water cantering down the cliff,
And here a shell to catch it with, and here
The round plump buns they gave me, and the fruit.
Now she is gone behind the rock.   O, rare
To be alone ! "   So Gladys sat her down,
Unpacked her little basket, ate and drank,
Then pushed her hands into the warm dry sand,
And thought the earth was happy, and she too
Was going round with it in happiness,
That holiday.   " What was it that she said ? "
Quoth Gladys, cogitating ; " they were kind,
The words that woman spoke.   She does not know !
' Her greater for their less,' — it makes me laugh, —
But yet," sighed Gladys, " though it must be good
To look and to admire, one should not wish
To steal THEIR virtues, and to put them on,
Like feathers from another wing ; beside,
That calm, and that grave consciousness of worth,
When all is said, would little suit with me,
Who am not worthy.   When our thoughts are born,
Though they be good and humble, one should mind
How they are reared, or some will go astray
And shame their mother.   Cain and Abel both
Were only once removed from innocence.

Why did I envy them?   That was not good;
Yet it began with my humility."

But as she spake, lo, Gladys raised her eyes,
And right before her, on the horizon's edge,
Behold, an island!   First, she looked away
Along the solid rocks and steadfast shore,
For she was all amazed, believing not,
And then she looked again, and there again
Behold, an island!   And the tide had turned,
The milky sea had got a purple rim,
And from the rim that mountain island rose,
Purple, with two high peaks, the northern peak
The higher, and with fell and precipice,
It ran down steeply to the water's brink;
But all the southern line was long and soft,
Broken with tender curves, and, as she thought,
Covered with forest or with sward.   But, look!
The sun was on the island; and he showed
On either peak a dazzling cap of snow.
Then Gladys held her breath; she said, " Indeed,
Indeed it is an island: how is this,
I never saw it till this fortunate
Rare holiday?"   And while she strained her eyes,
She thought that it began to fade; but not
To change as clouds do, only to withdraw
And melt into its azure; and at last,
Little by little, from her hungry heart,
That longed to draw things marvellous to itself,

And yearned towards the riches and the great
Abundance of the beauty God hath made,
It passed away. Tears started in her eyes,
And when they dropt, the mountain isle was gone;
The careless sea had quite forgotten it,
And all was even as it had been before.

And Gladys wept, but there was luxury
In her self-pity, while she softly sobbed,
" O, what a little while! I am afraid
I shall forget that purple mountain isle,
The lovely hollows atween her snow-clad peaks,
The grace of her upheaval where she lay
Well up against the open. O, my heart,
Now I remember how this holiday
Will soon be done, and now my life goes on
Not fed; and only in the noonday walk
Let to look silently at what it wants,
Without the power to wait or pause awhile,
And understand and draw within itself
The richness of the earth. A holiday!
How few I have! I spend the silent time
At work, while all THEIR pupils are gone home,
And feel myself remote. They shine apart;
They are great planets, I a little orb;
My little orbit far within their own
Turns, and approaches not. But yet, the more
I am alone when those I teach return;
For they, as planets of some other sun,

Not mine, have paths that can but meet my ring
Once in a cycle. O, how poor I am!
I have not got laid up in this blank heart
Any indulgent kisses given me
Because I had been good, or, yet more sweet,
Because my childhood was itself a good
Attractive thing for kisses, tender praise,
And comforting. An orphan-school at best
Is a cold mother in the winter time
('T was mostly winter when new orphans came),
An unregarded mother in the spring.

" Yet once a year (I did mine wrong) we went
To gather cowslips. How we thought on it
Beforehand, pacing, pacing the dull street,
To that one tree, the only one we saw
From April, — if the cowslips were in bloom
So early; or if not, from opening May
Even to September. Then there came the feast
At Epping. If it rained that day, it rained
For a whole year to us; we could not think
Of fields and hawthorn hedges, and the leaves
Fluttering, but still it rained, and ever rained.

" Ah, well, but I am here; but I have seen
The gay gorse bushes in their flowering time;
I know the scent of bean-fields; I have heard
The satisfying murmur of the main."

The woman!   She came round the rock again
With her fair baby, and she sat her down
By Gladys, murmuring, " Who forbade the grass
To grow by visitations of the dew ?
Who said in ancient time to the desert pool,
' Thou shalt not wait for angel visitors
To trouble thy still water ? '   Must we bide
At home ?   The lore, beloved, shall fly to us
On a pair of sumptuous wings.   Or may we breathe
Without ?   O, we shall draw to us the air
That times and mystery feed on.   This shall lay
Unchidden hands upon the heart o' the world,
And feel it beating.   Rivers shall run on,
Full of sweet language as a lover's mouth,
Delivering of a tune to make her youth
More beautiful than wheat when it is green.

" What else ? — (O, none shall envy her !)   The rain
And the wild weather will be most her own,
And talk with her o' nights ; and if the winds
Have seen aught wondrous, they will tell it her
In a mouthful of strange moans, — will bring from far,
Her ears being keen, the lowing and the mad
Masterful tramping of the bison herds,
Tearing down headlong with their bloodshot eyes,
In savage rifts of hair ; the crack and creak
Of ice-floes in the frozen sea, the cry
Of the white bears, all in a dim blue world
Mumbling their meals by twilight ; or the rock

And majesty of motion, when their heads
Primeval trees toss in a sunny storm,
And hail their nuts down on unweeded fields.
No holidays," quoth she ; " drop, drop, O, drop,
Thou tired skylark, and go up no more ;
You lime-trees, cover not your head with bees,
Nor give out your good smell.   She will not look ;
No, Gladys cannot draw your sweetness in,
For lack of holidays."   So Gladys thought,
" A most strange woman, and she talks of me."
With that a girl ran up ; " Mother," she said,
" Come out of this brown bight, I pray you now,
It smells of fairies."   Gladys thereon thought,
" The mother will not speak to me, perhaps
The daughter may," and asked her courteously,
" What do the fairies smell of ? "   But the girl
With peevish pout replied, " You know, you know."
" Not I," said Gladys ; then she answered her,
" Something like buttercups.   But, mother, come,
And whisper up a porpoise from the foam,
Because I want to ride."

                Full slowly, then,
The mother rose, and ever kept her eyes
Upon her little child.   " You freakish maid,"
Said she, " now mark me, if I call you one,
You shall not scold nor make him take you far."

" I only want, — you know I only want,"
The girl replied, " to go and play awhile

Upon the sand by Lagos." Then she turned
And muttered low, " Mother, is this the girl
Who saw the island ? " But the mother frowned.
" When may she go to it ? " the daughter asked.
And Gladys, following them, gave all her mind
To hear the answer. " When she wills to go ;
For yonder comes to shore the ferry boat."
Then Gladys turned to look, and even so
It was ; a ferry boat, and far away
Reared in the offing, lo, the purple peaks
Of her loved island.

     Then she raised her arms,
And ran toward the boat, crying out, " O rare,
The island ! fair befall the island ; let
Me reach the island." And she sprang on board,
And after her stepped in the freakish maid
And the fair mother, brooding o'er her child ;
And this one took the helm, and that let go
The sail, and off they flew, and furrowed up
A flaky hill before, and left behind
A sobbing snake-like tail of creamy foam ;
And dancing hither, thither, sometimes shot
Toward the island ; then, when Gladys looked,
Were leaving it to leeward. And the maid
Whistled a wind to come and rock the craft,
And would be leaning down her head to mew
At cat-fish, then lift out into her lap
And dandle baby-seals, which, having kissed,
She flung to their sleek mothers, till her own

Rebuked her in good English, after cried,
" Luff, luff, we shall be swamped."   " I will not luff,"
Sobbed the fair mischief; "you are cross to me."
" For shame!" the mother shrieked; "luff, luff, my
        dear ;
Kiss and be friends, and thou shalt have the fish
With the curly tail to ride on." So she did,
And presently a dolphin bouncing up,
She sprang upon his slippery back, — " Farewell,"
She laughed, was off, and all the sea grew calm.

Then Gladys was much happier, and was 'ware
In the smooth weather that this woman talked
Like one in sleep, and murmured certain thoughts
Which seemed to be like echoes of her own.
She nodded, " Yes, the girl is going now
To her own island.   Gladys poor? Not she !
Who thinks so?   Once I met a man in white,
Who said to me, 'The thing that might have been
Is called, and questioned why it hath not been ;
And can it give good reason, it is set
Beside the actual, and reckoned in
To fill the empty gaps of life.'   Ah, so
The possible stands by us ever fresh,
Fairer than aught which any life hath owned,
And makes divine amends.   Now this was set
Apart from kin, and not ordained a home ;
An equal ; — and not suffered to fence in
A little plot of earthly good, and say,

'T is mine'; but in bereavement of the part,
O, yet to taste the whole, — to understand
The grandeur of the story, not to feel
Satiate with good possessed, but evermore
A healthful hunger for the great idea,
The beauty and the blessedness of life.

" Lo, now, the shadow !" quoth she, breaking off,
" We are in the shadow."   Then did Gladys turn,
And, O, the mountain with the purple peaks
Was close at hand.   It cast a shadow out,
And they were in it : and she saw the snow,
And under that the rocks, and under that
The pines, and then the pasturage ; and saw
Numerous dips, and undulations rare,
Running down seaward, all astir with lithe
Long canes, and lofty feathers ; for the palms
And spice trees of the south, nay, every growth,
Meets in that island.
                        So that woman ran
The boat ashore, and Gladys set her foot
Thereon.   Then all at once much laughter rose ;
Invisible folk set up exultant shouts,
" It all belongs to Gladys "; and she ran
And hid herself among the nearest trees
And panted, shedding tears.
                        So she looked round,
And saw that she was in a banyan grove,
Full of wild peacocks, — pecking on the grass,

A flickering mass of eyes, blue, green, and gold,
Or reaching out their jewelled necks, where high
They sat in rows along the boughs. No tree
Cumbered with creepers let the sunshine through,
But it was caught in scarlet cups, and poured
From these on amber tufts of bloom, and dropped
Lower on azure stars. The air was still,
As if awaiting somewhat, or asleep,
And Gladys was the only thing that moved,
Excepting, — no, they were not birds, — what then?
Glorified rainbows with a living soul?
While they passed through a sunbeam they were seen,
Not otherwhere, but they were present yet
In shade. They were at work, pomegranate fruit
That lay about removing, — purple grapes,
That clustered in the path, clearing aside.
Through a small spot of light would pass and go,
The glorious happy mouth and two fair eyes
Of somewhat that made rustlings where it went;
But when a beam would strike the ground sheer down,
Behold them! they had wings, and they would pass
One after other with the sheeny fans,
Bearing them slowly, that their hues were seen,
Tender as russet crimson dropt on snows,
Or where they turned flashing with gold and dashed
With purple glooms. And they had feet, but these
Did barely touch the ground. And they took heed
Not to disturb the waiting quietness ;
Nor rouse up fawns, that slept beside their dams ;

Nor the fair leopard, with her sleek paws laid
Across her little drowsy cubs ; nor swans,
That, floating, slept upon a glassy pool ;
Nor rosy cranes, all slumbering in the reeds,
With heads beneath their wings.   For this, you know,
Was Eden.   She was passing through the trees
That made a ring about it, and she caught
A glimpse of glades beyond.   All she had seen
Was nothing to them ; but words are not made
To tell that tale.   No wind was let to blow,
And all the doves were bidden to hold their peace.
Why?   One was working in a valley near,
And none might look that way.   It was understood
That He had nearly ended that His work ;
For two shapes met, and one to other spake,
Accosting him with, " Prince, what worketh He ? "
Who whispered, " Lo ! He fashioneth red clay."
And all at once a little trembling stir
Was felt in the earth, and every creature woke,
And laid its head down, listening.   It was known
Then that the work was done ; the new-made king
Had risen, and set his feet upon his realm,
And it acknowledged him.
                              But in her path
Came some one that withstood her, and he said,
" What doest thou here ? "   Then she did turn and flee,
Among those colored spirits, through the grove,
Trembling for haste ; it was not well with her
Till she came forth of those thick banyan-trees,

And set her feet upon the common grass,
And felt the common wind.

                 Yet once beyond,
She could not choose but cast a backward glance.
The lovely matted growth stood like a wall,
And means of entering were not evident, —
The gap had closed. But Gladys laughed for joy ;
She said, " Remoteness and a multitude
Of years are counted nothing here. Behold,
To-day I have been in Eden. O, it blooms
In my own island."

                    And she wandered on,
Thinking, until she reached a place of palms,
And all the earth was sandy where she walked, —
Sandy and dry, — strewed with papyrus leaves,
Old idols, rings and pottery, painted lids
Of mummies (for perhaps is was the way
That leads to dead old Egypt), and withal
Excellent sunshine cut out sharp and clear
The hot prone pillars, and the carven plinths, —
Stone lotus cups, with petals dipped in sand,
And wicked gods, and sphinxes bland, who sat
And smiled upon the ruin. O how still !
Hot, blank, illuminated with the clear
Stare of an unveiled sky. The dry stiff leaves
Of palm-trees never rustled, and the soul
Of that dead ancientry was itself dead.
She was above her ankles in the sand,
When she beheld a rocky road, and, lo !

11   P

It bare in it the ruts of chariot wheels,
Which erst had carried to their pagan prayers
The brown old Pharaohs ; for the ruts led on
To a great cliff, that either was a cliff
Or some dread shrine in ruins, — partly reared
In front of that same cliff, and partly hewn
Or excavate within its heart.   Great heaps
Of sand and stones on either side there lay ;
And, as the girl drew on, rose out from each,
As from a ghostly kennel, gods unblest,
Dog-headed, and behind them wingéd things
Like angels ; and this carven multitude
Hedged in, to right and left, the rocky road.

 At last, the cliff, — and in the cliff a door
Yawning : and she looked in, as down the throat
Of some stupendous giant, and beheld
No floor, but wide, worn, flights of steps, that led
Into a dimness.   When the eyes could bear
That change to gloom, she saw flight after flight,
Flight after flight, the worn long stair go down,
Smooth with the feet of nations dead and gone.
So she did enter ; also she went down
Till it was dark, and yet again went down,
Till, gazing upward at that yawning door,
It seemed no larger, in its height remote,
Than a pin's head.   But while, irresolute,
She doubted of the end, yet farther down
A slender ray of lamplight fell away
Along the stair, as from a door ajar :

To this again she felt her way, and stepped
Adown the hollow stair, and reached the light ;
But fear fell on her, fear ; and she forbore
Entrance, and listened.   Ay ! 't was even so, —
A sigh ; the breathing as of one who slept
And was disturbed.   So she drew back awhile,
And trembled ; then her doubting hand she laid
Against the door, and pushed it ; but the light
Waned, faded, sank ; and as she came within —
Hark, hark !   A spirit was it, and asleep ?
A spirit doth not breathe like clay.   There hung
A cresset from the roof, and thence appeared
A flickering speck of light, and disappeared ;
Then dropped along the floor its elfish flakes,
That fell on some one resting, in the gloom, —
Somewhat, a spectral shadow, then a shape
That loomed.   It was a heifer, ay, and white,
Breathing and languid through prolonged repose.

   Was it a heifer ? all the marble floor
Was milk-white also, and the cresset paled,
And straight their whiteness grew confused and mixed.

   But when the cresset, taking heart, bloomed out, —
The whiteness, — and asleep again ! but now
It was a woman, robed, and with a face
Lovely and dim.   And Gladys while she gazed
Murmured, " O terrible !   I am afraid
To breathe among these intermittent lives,

That fluctuate in mystic solitude,
And change and fade. Lo! where the goddess sits
Dreaming on her dim throne; a crescent moon
She wears upon her forehead. Ah! her frown
Is mournful, and her slumber is not sweet.
What dost thou hold, Isis, to thy cold breast?
A baby god with finger on his lips,
Asleep, and dreaming of departed sway?
Thy son. Hush, hush; he knoweth all the lore
And sorcery of old Egypt; but his mouth
He shuts; the secret shall be lost with him,
He will not tell."

     The woman coming down!
" Child, what art doing here?" the woman said;
" What wilt thou of Dame Isis and her bairn?"
(*Ay, ay, we see thee breathing in thy shroud, —*
Thy pretty shroud, all frilled and furbelowed.)
The air is dim with dust of spicéd bones.
I mark a crypt down there. Tier upon tier
Of painted coffers fills it. What if we,
Passing, should slip, and crash into their midst, —
Break the frail ancientry, and smothered lie,
Tumbled among the ribs of queens and kings,
And all the gear they took to bed with them!
Horrible! Let us hence.

     And Gladys said,
" O, they are rough to mount, those stairs"; but she
Took her and laughed, and up the mighty flight
Shot like a meteor with her. " There," said she;

" The light is sweet when one has smelled of graves,
Down in unholy heathen gloom ; farewell."
She pointed to a gateway, strong and high,
Reared of hewn stones ; but, look ! in lieu of gate,
There was a glittering cobweb drawn across,
And on the lintel there were writ these words:
" Ho, every one that cometh, I divide
What hath been from what might be, and the line
Hangeth before thee as a spider's web ;
Yet, wouldst thou enter thou must break the line,
Or else forbear the hill."

                 The maiden said,
" So, cobweb, I will break thee."   And she passed
Among some oak-trees on the farther side,
And waded through the bracken round their bolls,
Until she saw the open, and drew on
Toward the edge o' the wood, where it was mixed
With pines and heathery places wild and fresh.
Here she put up a creature, that ran on
Before her, crying, " Tint, tint, tint," and turned,
Sat up, and stared at her with elfish eyes,
Jabbering of gramarye, one Michael Scott,
The wizard that wonned somewhere underground,
With other talk enough to make one fear
To walk in lonely places.   After passed
A man-at-arms, William of Deloraine ;
He shook his head, " An' if I list to tell,"
Quoth he, " I know, but how it matters not " ;
Then crossed himself, and muttered of a clap

Of thunder, and a shape in Amice gray,
But still it mouthed at him, and whimpered, " Tint,
Tint, tint." " There shall be wild work some day soon,"
Quoth he, " thou limb of darkness: he will come,
Thy master, push a hand up, catch thee, imp,
And so good Christians shall have peace, perdie."

Then Gladys was so frightened, that she ran,
And got away, towards a grassy down,
Where sheep and lambs were feeding, with a boy
To tend them. 'T was the boy who wears that herb
Called heart's-ease in his bosom, and he sang
So sweetly to his flock, that she stole on
Nearer to listen. " O Content, Content,
Give me," sang he, " thy tender company.
I feed my flock among the myrtles; all
My lambs are twins, and they have laid them down
Along the slopes of Beulah. Come, fair love,
From the other side the river, where their harps
Thou hast been helping them to tune. O come,
And pitch thy tent by mine; let me behold
Thy mouth, — that even in slumber talks of peace, —
Thy well-set locks, and dove-like countenance."

And Gladys hearkened, couched upon the grass,
Till she had rested; then did ask the boy,
For it was afternoon, and she was fain
To reach the shore, " Which is the path, I pray,
That leads one to the water?" But he said,

" Dear lass, I only know the narrow way,
The path that leads one to the golden gate
Across the river."   So she wandered on ;
And presently her feet grew cool, the grass
Standing so high, and thyme being thick and soft.
The air was full of voices, and the scent
Of mountain blossom loaded all its wafts ;
For she was on the slopes of a goodly mount,
And reared in such a sort that it looked down
Into the deepest valleys, darkest glades,
And richest plains o' the island.   It was set
Midway between the snows majestical
And a wide level, such as men would choose
For growing wheat ; and some one said to her,
" It is the hill Parnassus."   So she walked
Yet on its lower slope, and she could hear
The calling of an unseen multitude
To some upon the mountain, " Give us more ";
And others said, " We are tired of this old world :
Make it look new again."   Then there were some
Who answered lovingly — (the dead yet speak
From that high mountain, as the living do) ;
But others sang desponding, " We have kept
The vision for a chosen few : we love
Fit audience better than a rough huzza
From the unreasoning crowd."
                              Then words came up :
" There was a time, you poets, was a time
When all the poetry was ours, and made

By some who climbed the mountain from our midst.
We loved it then, we sang it in our streets.
O, it grows obsolete!   Be you as they:
Our heroes die and drop away from us;
Oblivion folds them 'neath her dusky wing,
Fair copies wasted to the hungering world.
Save them.   We fall so low for lack of them,
That many of us think scorn of honest trade,
And take no pride in our own shops; who care
Only to quit a calling, will not make
The calling what it might be; who despise
Their work, Fate laughs at, and doth let the work
Dull, and degrade them."
                        Then did Gladys smile:
" Heroes!" quoth she; "yet, now I think on it,
There was the jolly goldsmith, brave Sir Hugh,
Certes, a hero ready-made.   Methinks
I see him burnishing of golden gear,
Tankard and charger, and a-muttering low,
' London is thirsty ' — (then he weighs a chain):
' 'T is an ill thing, my masters.   I would give
The worth of this, and many such as this,
To bring it water.'
                        " Ay, and after him
There came up Guy of London, lettered son
O' the honest lighterman.   I 'll think on him,
Leaning upon the bridge on summer eves,
After his shop was closed: a still, grave man,
With melancholy eyes.   ' While these are hale,'

He saith, when he looks down and marks the crowd
Cheerily working ; where the river marge
Is blocked with ships and boats ; and all the wharves
Swarm, and the cranes swing in with merchandise, —
' While these are hale, 't is well, 't is very well.
But, O good Lord,' saith he, ' when these are sick, —
I fear me, Lord, this excellent workmanship
Of Thine is counted for a cumbrance then.
Ay, ay, my hearties ! many a man of you,
Struck down, or maimed, or fevered, shrinks away,
And, mastered in that fight for lack of aid,
Creeps shivering to a corner, and there dies.'
Well, we have heard the rest.

                     " Ah, next I think
Upon the merchant captain, stout of heart
To dare and to endure. ' Robert,' saith he,
(The navigator Knox to his manful son,)
' I sit a captive from the ship detained ;
This heathenry doth let thee visit her.
Remember, son, if thou, alas ! shouldst fail
To ransom thy poor father, they are free
As yet, the mariners ; have wives at home,
As I have ; ay, and liberty is sweet
To all men. For the ship, she is not ours,
Therefore, 'beseech thee, son, lay on the mate
This my command, to leave me, and set sail.
As for thyself —' ' Good father,' saith the son ;
' I will not, father, ask your blessing now,
Because, for fair, or else for evil, fate

11*

We two shall meet again.'   And so they did.
The dusky men, peeling off cinnamon,
And beating nutmeg clusters from the tree,
Ransom and bribe contemned.   The good ship sailed, —
The son returned to share his father's cell.

" O, there are many such.   Would I had wit
Their worth to sing ! "   With that, she turned her feet.
" I am tired now," said Gladys, " of their talk
Around this hill Parnassus."   And, behold,
A piteous sight — an old, blind, graybeard king
Led by a fool with bells.   Now this was loved
Of the crowd below the hill ; and when he called
For his lost kingdom, and bewailed his age,
And plained on his unkind daughters, they were known
To say, that if the best of gold and gear
Could have bought him back his kingdom, and made
        kind
The hard hearts which had broken his erewhile,
They would have gladly paid it from their store
Many times over.   What is done is done,
No help.   The ruined majesty passed on.
And look you ! one who met her as she walked
Showed her a mountain nymph lovely as light.
Her name Œnone ; and she mourned and mourned,
" O Mother Ida," and she could not cease,
No, nor be comforted.
                        And after this,
Soon there came by, arrayed in Norman cap

And kirtle, an Arcadian villager,
Who said, " I pray you, have you chanced to meet
One Gabriel?" and she sighed ; but Gladys took
And kissed her hand : she could not answer her,
Because she guessed the end.

      With that it drew
To evening ; and as Gladys wandered on
In the calm weather, she beheld the wave,
And she ran down to set her feet again
On the sea margin, which was covered thick
With white shell-skeletons. The sky was red
As wine. The water played among bare ribs
Of many wrecks, that lay half buried there
In the sand. She saw a cave, and moved thereto
To ask her way, and one so innocent
Came out to meet her, that, with marvelling mute,
She gazed and gazed into her sea-blue eyes,
For in them beamed the untaught ecstasy
Of childhood, that lives on though youth be come,
And love just born.

She could not choose but name her shipwrecked prince,
All blushing. She told Gladys many things
That are not in the story, — things, in sooth,
That Prospero her father knew. But now
'T was evening, and the sun drooped ; purple stripes
In the sea were copied from some clouds that lay
Out in the west. And lo ! the boat, and more,
The freakish thing to take fair Gladys home

She mowed at her, but Gladys took the helm:
Peace, peace !" she said ; " be good: you shall not steer,
For I am your liege lady." Then she sang
The sweetest songs she knew all the way home.

So Gladys set her feet upon the sand ;
While in the sunset glory died away
The peaks of that blest island.
                                        " Fare you well.
My country, my own kingdom," then she said,
" Till I go visit you again, farewell."

She looked toward their house with whom she dwelt, —
The carriages were coming. Hastening up,
She was in time to meet them at the door,
And lead the sleepy little ones within ;
And some were cross and shivered, and her dames
Were weary and right hard to please ; but she
Felt like a beggar suddenly endowed
With a warm cloak to 'fend her from the cold.
" For, come what will," she said, " I had *to-day.*
There is an island."

The Moral.

What is the moral? Let us think awhile,
Taking the editorial WE to help,
It sounds respectable.
                            The moral; yes.

We always read, when any fable ends,
" Hence we may learn." A moral must be found.
What do you think of this? " Hence we may learn
That dolphins swim about the coast of Wales,
And Admiralty maps should now be drawn
By teacher-girls, because their sight is keen,
And they can spy out islands." Will that do?
No, that is far too plain, — too evident.

Perhaps a general moralizing vein —
(We know we have a happy knack that way.
We have observed, moreover, that young men
Are fond of good advice, and so are girls ;
Especially of that meandering kind,
Which winding on so sweetly, treats of all
They ought to be and do and think and wear,
As one may say, from creeds to comforters.
Indeed, we much prefer that sort ourselves,
So soothing). Good, a moralizing vein ;
That is the thing ; but how to manage it ?
" *Hence we may learn,*" if we be so inclined,
That life goes best with those who take it best ;
That wit can spin from work a golden robe
To queen it in ; that who can paint at will
A private picture gallery, should not cry
For shillings that will let him in to look
At some by others painted. Furthermore,
Hence we may learn, you poets, — (*and we count
For poets all who ever felt that such*

They were, and all who secretly have known
That such they could be; ay, moreover, all
Who wind the robes of ideality
About the bareness of their lives, and hang
Comforting curtains, knit of fancy's yarn,
Nightly betwixt them and the frosty world), —
Hence we may learn, you poets, that of all
We should be most content. The earth is given
To us: we reign by virtue of a sense
Which lets us hear the rhythm of that old verse,
The ring of that old tune 'whereto she spins.
Humanity is given to us: we reign
By virtue of a sense, which lets us in
To know its troubles ere they have been told,
And take them home and lull them into rest
With mournfullest music. Time is given to us, —
Time past, time future. Who, good sooth, beside
Have seen it well, have walked this empty world
When she went steaming, and from pulpy hills
Have marked the spurting of their flamy crowns?

Have we not seen the tabernacle pitched,
And peered between the linen curtains, blue,
Purple, and scarlet, at the dimness there,
And, frighted, have not dared to look again?
But, quaint antiquity! beheld, we thought,
A chest that might have held the manna pot
And Aaron's rod that budded. Ay, we leaned
Over the edge of Britain, while the fleet

Of Cæsar loomed and neared ; then, afterwards,
We saw fair Venice looking at herself
In the glass below her, while her Doge went forth
In all his bravery to the wedding.

                               This,
However, counts for nothing to the grace
We wot of in time future : — therefore add,
And afterwards have done : " *Hence we may learn,*"
That though it be a grand and comely thing
To be unhappy, — (and we think it is,
Because so many grand and clever folk
Have found out reasons for unhappiness,
And talked about uncomfortable things, —
Low motives, bores, and shams, and hollowness,
The hollowness o' the world, till we at last
Have scarcely dared to jump or stamp, for fear,
Being so hollow, it should break some day,
And let us in), — yet, since we are not grand,
O, not at all, and as for cleverness,
That may be or may not be, — it is well
For us to be as happy as we can !

Agreed ; and with a word to the nobler sex,
As thus ; we pray you carry not your guns
On the half-cock ; we pray you set your pride
In its proper place, and never be ashamed
Of any honest calling, — let us add,
And end ; for all the rest, hold up your heads
And mind your English.

SONGS WITH PRELUDES.

Q

WEDLOCK.

THE sun was streaming in : I woke, and said,
    " Where is my wife, — that has been made my
            wife
Only this year ? " The casement stood ajar :
I did but lift my head : The pear-tree dropped,
The great white pear-tree dropped with dew from leaves
And blossom, under heavens of happy blue.

My wife had wakened first, and had gone down
Into the orchard. All the air was calm ;
Audible humming filled it. At the roots
Of peony bushes lay in rose-red heaps,
Or snowy, fallen bloom. The crag-like hills
Were tossing down their silver messengers,
And two brown foreigners, called cuckoo-birds,
Gave them good answer ; all things else were mute ;
An idle world lay listening to their talk,
They had it to themselves.

                    What ails my wife?
I know not if aught ails her; though her step
Tell of a conscious quiet, lest I wake.
She moves atween the almond boughs, and bends
One thick with bloom to look on it.   "O love!
A little while thou hast withdrawn thyself,
At unaware to think thy thoughts alone:
How sweet, and yet pathetic to my heart
The reason.   Ah! thou art no more thine own.
Mine, mine, O love!   Tears gather 'neath my lids, —
Sorrowful tears for thy lost liberty,
Because it was so sweet.   Thy liberty,
That yet, O love, thou wouldst not have again.
No; all is right.   But who can give, or bless,
Or take a blessing, but there comes withal
Some pain?"
                    She walks beside the lily bed,
And holds apart her gown; she would not hurt
The leaf-enfolded buds, that have not looked
Yet on the daylight.   O, thy locks are brown, —
Fairest of colors! — and a darker brown
The beautiful, dear, veiléd, modest eyes.
A bloom as of blush roses covers her
Forehead, and throat, and cheek.   Health breathes with
        her,
And graceful vigor.   Fair and wondrous soul!
To think that thou art mine!
                    My wife came in,
And moved into the chamber.   As for me,

I heard, but lay as one that nothing hears,
And feigned to be asleep.

I.

The racing river leaped, and sang
    Full blithely in the perfect weather,
All round the mountain echoes rang,
    For blue and green were glad together.

II.

This rained out light from every part,
    And that with songs of joy was thrilling;
But, in the hollow of my heart,
    There ached a place that wanted filling.

III.

Before the road and river meet,
    And stepping-stones are wet and glisten,
I heard a sound of laughter sweet,
    And paused to like it, and to listen.

IV.

I heard the chanting waters flow,
    The cushat's note, the bee's low humming, —
Then turned the hedge, and did not know, —
    How could I ? — that my time was coming.

V.

A girl upon the nighest stone,
    Half doubtful of the deed, was standing,
So far the shallow flood had flown
    Beyond the 'customed leap of landing.

VI.

She knew not any need of me,
    Yet me she waited all unweeting;
We thought not I had crossed the sea,
    And half the sphere to give her meeting.

VII.

I waded out, her eyes I met,
    I wished the moment had been hours;
I took her in my arms, and set
    Her dainty feet among the flowers.

VIII.

Her fellow maids in copse and lane,
    Ah! still, methinks, I hear them calling;
The wind's soft whisper in the plain,
    The cushat's coo, the water's falling.

IX.

But now it is a year ago,
 But now possession crowns endeavor;
I took her in my heart, to grow
 And fill the hollow place forever.

REGRET.

O THAT word REGRET!
 There have been nights and morns when we have
  sighed,
"Let us alone, Regret! We are content
To throw thee all our past, so thou wilt sleep
For aye." But it is patient, and it wakes;
It hath not learned to cry itself to sleep,
But plaineth on the bed that it is hard.

We did amiss when we did wish it gone
And over: sorrows humanize our race;
Tears are the showers that fertilize this world;
And memory of things precious keepeth warm
The heart that once did hold them.
       They are poor
That have lost nothing; they are poorer far
Who, losing, have forgotten; they most poor
Of all, who lose and wish they MIGHT forget.

For life is one, and in its warp and woof
There runs a thread of gold that glitters fair,
And sometimes in the pattern shows most sweet
Where there are sombre colors.   It is true
That we have wept.   But O ! this thread of gold,
We would not have it tarnish ; let us turn
Oft and look back upon the wondrous web,
And when it shineth sometimes we shall know
That memory is possession.

I.

When I remember something which I had,
   But which is gone, and I must do without,
I sometimes wonder how I can be glad,
   Even in cowslip time when hedges sprout ;
It makes me sigh to think on it, — but yet
My days will not be better days, should I forget.

II.

When I remember something promised me,
   But which I never had, nor can have now,
Because the promiser we no more see
   In countries that accord with mortal vow ;
When I remember this, I mourn, — but yet
My happier days are not the days when I forget.

LAMENTATION.

I READ upon that book,
  Which down the golden gulf doth let us look
On the sweet days of pastoral majesty;
    I read upon that book
    How, when the Shepherd Prince did flee
    (Red Esau's twin), he desolate took
The stone for a pillow: then he fell on sleep.
And lo! there was a ladder. Lo! there hung
A ladder from the star-place, and it clung
To the earth: it tied her so to heaven; and O!
    There fluttered wings;
Then were ascending and descending things
    That stepped to him where he lay low;
Then up the ladder would a-drifting go
(This feathered brood of heaven), and show
Small as white flakes in winter that are blown
Together, underneath the great white throne.

    When I had shut the book, I said,
" Now, as for me, my dreams upon my bed
    Are not like Jacob's dream;
Yet I have got it in my life; yes, I,
And many more: it doth not us beseem,
    Therefore, to sigh.
Is there not hung a ladder in our sky?
12

Yea; and, moreover, all the way up on high
Is thickly peopled with the prayers of men.
　　　We have no dream!　What then?
Like wingéd wayfarers the height they scale
(By Him that offers them they shall prevail), —
　　　The prayers of men.
　　　But where is found a prayer for me;
　　　How should I pray?
　　　My heart is sick, and full of strife.
I heard one whisper with departing breath,
' Suffer us not, for any pains of death,
　　　To fall from Thee.'
But O, the pains of life! the pains of life!
　　　There is no comfort now, and naught to win,
　　　But yet, — I will begin."

I.

" Preserve to me my wealth," I do not say,
　　　For that is wasted away;
And much of it was cankered ere it went.
" Preserve to me my health," I cannot say,
　　　For that, upon a day,
Went after other delights to banishment.

II.

What can I pray? " Give me forgetfulness "?
　　　No, I would still possess

Past away smiles, though present fronts be stern.
" Give me again my kindred?"   Nay; not so,
             Not idle prayers.   We know
They that have crossed the river cannot return.

III.

I do not pray, " Comfort me! comfort me!"
             For how should comfort be?
O, — O that cooing mouth, — that little white head!
No; but I pray, " If it be not too late,
             Open to me the gate,
That I may find my babe when I am dead.

IV.

" Show me the path.   I had forgotten Thee
             When I was happy and free,
Walking down here in the gladsome light o' the sun;
But now I come and mourn; O set my feet
             In the road to Thy blest seat,
And for the rest, O God, Thy will be done."

WHEN found the rose delight in her fair hue?
  Color is nothing to this world; 't is I
That see it.   Farther, I discover soul,
That trees are nothing to their fellow trees;
It is but I that love their stateliness,
And I that, comforting my heart, do sit
At noon beneath their shadow.   I will step
On the ledges of this world, for it is mine;
But the other world ye wot of, shall go too;
I will carry it in my bosom.   O my world,
That was not built with clay!

                        Consider it
(This outer world we tread on) as a harp, —
A gracious instrument on whose fair strings
We learn those airs we shall be set to play
When mortal hours are ended.   Let the wings,
Man, of thy spirit move on it as wind,
And draw forth melody.   Why shouldst thou yet
Lie grovelling?   More is won than e'er was lost:
Inherit.   Let thy day be to thy night
A teller of good tidings.   Let thy praise
Go up as birds go up that, when they wake,
Shake off the dew and soar.

                        So take Joy home,
And make a place in thy great heart for her,

And give her time to grow, and cherish her;
Then will she come, and oft will sing to thee,
When thou art working in the furrows; ay,
Or weeding in the sacred hour of dawn.
It is a comely fashion to be glad, —
Joy is the grace we say to God.

       Art tired?
There is a rest remaining. Hast thou sinned?
There is a Sacrifice. Lift up thy head,
The lovely world, and the over-world alike,
Ring with a song eterne, a happy rede,
" THY FATHER LOVES THEE."

I.

Yon moorèd mackerel fleet
 Hangs thick as a swarm of bees,
Or a clustering village street
 Foundationless built on the seas.

II.

The mariners ply their craft,
 Each set in his castle frail;
His care is all for the draught,
 And he dries the rain-beaten sail.

III.

For rain came down in the night,
 And thunder muttered full oft,

But now the azure is bright,
　　And hawks are wheeling aloft.

IV.

I take the land to my breast,
　　In her coat with daisies fine;
For me are the hills in their best,
　　And all that's made is mine.

V.

Sing high! "Though the red sun dip,
　　There yet is a day for me;
Nor youth I count for a ship
　　That long ago foundered at sea.

VI.

" Did the lost love die and depart?
　　Many times since we have met;
For I hold the years in my heart,
　　And all that was — is yet.

VII.

" I grant to the king his reign;
　　Let us yield him homage due;
But over the lands there are twain,
　　O king, I must rule as you.

VIII.

" I grant to the wise his meed,
    But his yoke I will not brook,
For God taught ME to read, —
    He lent me the world for a book."

FRIENDSHIP.

ON A SUN-PORTRAIT OF HER HUSBAND, SENT BY HIS WIFE TO THEIR FRIEND.

BEAUTIFUL eyes, — and shall I see no more
    The living thought when it would leap from them,
And play in all its sweetness 'neath their lids ?

Here was a man familiar with fair heights
That poets climb.   Upon his peace the tears
And troubles of our race deep inroads made,
Yet life was sweet to him ; he kept his heart
At home.   Who saw his wife might well have thought, —
" God loves this man.   He chose a wife for him, —
The true one ! "   O sweet eyes, that seem to live,
I know so much of you, tell me the rest !
Eyes full of fatherhood and tender care
For small, young children.   Is a message here
That you would fain have sent, but had not time ?

If such there be, I promise, by long love
And perfect friendship, by all trust that comes
Of understanding, that I will not fail,
No, nor delay to find it.

        O, my heart
Will often pain me as for some strange fault, —
Some grave defect in nature, — when I think
How I, delighted, 'neath those olive-trees,
Moved to the music of the tideless main,
While, with sore weeping, in an island home
They laid that much-loved head beneath the sod,
And I did not know.

I.

I stand on the bridge where last we stood
    When delicate leaves were young;
The children called us from yonder wood,
    While a mated blackbird sung.

II.

Ah, yet you call, — in your gladness call, —
    And I hear your pattering feet;
It does not matter, matter at all,
    You fatherless children sweet, —

III.

It does not matter at all to you,
    Young hearts that pleasure besets;

The father sleeps, but the world is new,
    The child of his love forgets.

IV.

I too, it may be, before they drop,
    The leaves that flicker to-day,
Ere bountiful gleams make ripe the crop,
    Shall pass from my place away :

V.

Ere yon gray cygnet puts on her white,
    Or snow lies soft on the wold,
Shall shut these eyes on the lovely light,
    And leave the story untold.

VI.

Shall I tell it there ?   Ah, let that be,
    For the warm pulse beats so high ;
To love to-day, and to breathe and see, —
    To-morrow perhaps to die, —

VII.

Leave it with God.   But this I have known,
    That sorrow is over soon ;
Some in dark nights, sore weeping alone,
    Forget by full of the moon.

12*   R

VIII.

But if all loved, as the few can love,
    This world would seldom be well;
And who need wish, if he dwells above,
    For a deep, a long death knell.

IX.

There are four or five, who, passing this place,
    While they live will name me yet;
And when I am gone will think on my face,
    And feel a kind of regret.

WINSTANLEY.

THE APOLOGY.

QUOTH the cedar to the reeds and rushes,
  " Water-grass, you know not what I do ;
Know not of my storms, nor of my hushes,
  And — I know not you."

Quoth the reeds and rushes, " Wind ! O waken !
  Breathe, O wind, and set our answer free,
For we have no voice, of you forsaken,
  For the cedar-tree."

Quoth the earth at midnight to the ocean,
  " Wilderness of water, lost to view,
Naught you are to me but sounds of motion ;
  I am naught to you."

Quoth the ocean, " Dawn ! O fairest, clearest,
  Touch me with thy golden fingers bland ;
For I have no smile till thou appearest
  For the lovely land."

Quoth the hero dying, whelmed in glory,
　" Many blame me, few have understood ;
Ah, my folk, to you I leave a story, —
　　　　Make its meaning good."

Quoth the folk, " Sing, poet ! teach us, prove us ;
　Surely we shall learn the meaning then ;
Wound us with a pain divine, O move us,
　　　　For this man of men."

―――――

WINSTANLEY'S deed, you kindly folk,
　　With it I fill my lay,
And a nobler man ne'er walked the world,
　　Let his name be what it may.

The good ship " Snowdrop " tarried long,
　　Up at the vane looked he ;
" Belike," he said, for the wind had dropped,
　　" She lieth becalmed at sea."

The lovely ladies flocked within,
　　And still would each one say,
" Good mercer, be the ships come up ? "
　　But still he answered " Nay."

Then stepped two mariners down the street,
　　With looks of grief and fear :
"Now, if Winstanley be your name,
　　We bring you evil cheer !

"For the good ship 'Snowdrop' struck, — she struck
    On the rock, — the Eddystone,
And down she went with threescore men,
    We two being left alone.

" Down in the deep, with freight and crew,
    Past any help she lies,
And never a bale has come to shore
    Of all thy merchandise."

" For cloth o' gold and comely frieze,"
    Winstanley said, and sighed,
" For velvet coif, or costly coat,
    They fathoms deep may bide.

" O thou brave skipper, blithe and kind,
    O mariners, bold and true,
Sorry at heart, right sorry am I,
    A-thinking of yours and you.

" Many long days Winstanley's breast
    Shall feel a weight within,
For a waft of wind he shall be 'feared
    And trading count but sin.

" To him no more it shall be joy
    To pace the cheerful town,
And see the lovely ladies gay
    Step on in velvet gown."

13

The " Snowdrop " sank at Lammas tide,
   All under the yeasty spray;
On Christmas Eve the brig " Content "
   Was also cast away.

He little thought o' New Year's night,
   So jolly as he sat then,
While drank the toast and praised the roast
   The round-faced Aldermen, —

While serving lads ran to and fro,
   Pouring the ruby wine,
And jellies trembled on the board,
   And towering pasties fine, —

While loud huzzas ran up the roof
   Till the lamps did rock o'erhead,
And holly-boughs from rafters hung
   Dropped down their berries red, —

He little thought on Plymouth Hoe,
   With every rising tide,
How the wave washed in his sailor-lads,
   And laid them side by side.

There stepped a stranger to the board:
   " Now, stranger, who be ye ? "
He looked to right, he looked to left,
   And " Rest you merry," quoth he ;

" For you did not see the brig go down,
　　Or ever a storm had blown ;
For you did not see the white wave rear
　　At the rock, — the Eddystone.

" She drave at the rock with sternsails set ;
　　Crash went the masts in twain ;
She staggered back with her mortal blow,
　　Then leaped at it again.

" There rose a great cry, bitter and strong,
　　The misty moon looked out !
And the water swarmed with seamen's heads,
　　And the wreck was strewed about.

" I saw her mainsail lash the sea
　　As I clung to the rock alone ;
Then she heeled over, and down she went,
　　And sank like any stone.

" She was a fair ship, but all 's one !
　　For naught could bide the shock."
" I will take horse," Winstanley said,
　　" And see this deadly rock."

" For never again shall bark o' mine
　　Sail over the windy sea,
Unless, by the blessing of God, for this
　　Be found a remedy."

Winstanley rode to Plymouth town
　　All in the sleet and the snow,
And he looked around on shore and sound
　　As he stood on Plymouth Hoe.

Till a pillar of spray rose far away,
　　And shot up its stately head,
Reared and fell over, and reared again :
　　" 'T is the rock ! the rock ! " he said.

Straight to the Mayor he took his way,
　　" Good Master Mayor," quoth he,
" I am a mercer of London town,
　　And owner of vessels three, —

" But for your rock of dark renown,
　　I had five to track the main."
" You are one of many," the old Mayor said,
　　" That on the rock complain.

" An ill rock, mercer ! your words ring right,
　　Well with my thoughts they chime,
For my two sons to the world to come
　　It sent before their time."

" Lend me a lighter, good Master Mayor,
　　And a score of shipwrights free,
For I think to raise a lantern tower
　　On this rock o' destiny."

The old Mayor laughed, but sighed also ;
   " Ah, youth," quoth he, " is rash ;
Sooner, young man, thou 'lt root it out
   From the sea that doth it lash.

" Who sails too near its jagged teeth,
   He shall have evil lot ;
For the calmest seas that tumble there
   Froth like a boiling pot.

And the heavier seas few look on nigh,
   But straight they lay him dead ;
A seventy-gun-ship, sir ! — they 'll shoot
   Higher than her mast-head.

" O, beacons sighted in the dark,
   They are right welcome things,
And pitchpots flaming on the shore
   Show fair as angel wings.

" Hast gold in hand ? then light the land,
   It 'longs to thee and me ;
But let alone the deadly rock
   In God Almighty's sea."

Yet said he, " Nay, — I must away,
   On the rock to set my feet ;
My debts are paid, my will I made,
   Or ever I did thee greet.

" If I must die, then let me die
 By the rock and not elsewhere ;
If I may live, O let me live
 To mount my lighthouse stair."

The old Mayor looked him in the face,
 And answered, " Have thy way ;
Thy heart is stout, as if round about
 It was braced with an iron stay :

" Have thy will, mercer ! choose thy men,
 Put off from the storm-rid shore ;
God with thee be, or I shall see
 Thy face and theirs no more."

Heavily plunged the breaking wave,
 And foam flew up the lea,
Morning and even the drifted snow
 Fell into the dark gray sea.

Winstanley chose him men and gear ;
 He said, " My time I waste,"
For the seas ran seething up the shore,
 And the wrack drave on in haste.

But twenty days he waited and more,
 Pacing the strand alone,
Or ever he sat his manly foot
 On the rock, — the Eddystone.

Then he and the sea began their strife,
  And worked with power and might:
Whatever the man reared up by day
  The sea broke down by night.

He wrought at ebb with bar and beam,
  He sailed to shore at flow;
And at his side, by that same tide,
  Came bar and beam also.

" Give in, give in," the old Mayor cried,
  " Or thou wilt rue the day."
" Yonder he goes," the townsfolk sighed,
  " But the rock will have its way.

" For all his looks that are so stout,
  And his speeches brave and fair,
He may wait on the wind, wait on the wave,
  But he 'll build no lighthouse there."

In fine weather and foul weather
  The rock his arts did flout,
Through the long days and the short days,
  Till all that year ran out.

With fine weather and foul weather
  Another year came in;
" To take his wage," the workmen said,
  " We almost count a sin."

Now March was gone, came April in,
    And a sea-fog settled down,
And forth sailed he on a glassy sea,
    He sailed from Plymouth town.

With men and stores he put to sea,
    As he was wont to do;
They showed in the fog like ghosts full faint, —
    A ghostly craft and crew.

And the sea-fog lay and waxed alway,
    For a long eight days and more;
" God help our men," quoth the women then;
    " For they bide long from shore."

They paced the Hoe in doubt and dread:
    " Where may our mariners be ? "
But the brooding fog lay soft as down
    Over the quiet sea.

A Scottish schooner made the port,
    The thirteenth day at e'en ;
" As I am a man," the captain cried,
    " A strange sight I have seen:

" And a strange sound heard, my masters all,
    At sea, in the fog and the rain,
Like shipwrights' hammers tapping low,
    Then loud, then low again.

" And a stately house one instant showed,
　　Through a rift, on the vessel's lee ;
What manner of creatures may be those
　　That build upon the sea ? "

Then sighed the folk, " The Lord be praised ! "
　　And they flocked to the shore amain ;
All over the Hoe that livelong night,
　　Many stood out in the rain.

It ceased, and the red sun reared his head,
　　And the rolling fog did flee ;
And, lo ! in the offing faint and far
　　Winstanley's house at sea !

In fair weather with mirth and cheer
　　The stately tower uprose ;
In foul weather, with hunger and cold,
　　They were content to close ;

Till up the stair Winstanley went,
　　To fire the wick afar ;
And Plymouth in the silent night
　　Looked out, and saw her star.

Winstanley set his foot ashore ;
　　Said he, " My work is done ;
I hold it strong to last as long
　　As aught beneath the sun.

" But if it fail, as fail it may,
　　Borne down with ruin and rout,
Another than I shall rear it high,
　　And brace the girders stout.

" A better than I shall rear it high,
　　For now the way is plain,
And tho' I were dead," Winstanley said,
　　" The light would shine again.

" Yet, were I fain still to remain,
　　Watch in my tower to keep,
And tend my light in the stormiest night
　　That ever did move the deep ;

" And if it stood, why then 't were good,
　　Amid their tremulous stirs,
To count each stroke when the mad waves broke,
　　For cheers of mariners.

" But if it fell, then this were well,
　　That I should with it fall ;
Since, for my part, I have built my heart
　　In the courses of its wall.

" Ay ! I were fain, long to remain,
　　Watch in my tower to keep,
And tend my light in the stormiest night
　　That ever did move the deep."

With that Winstanley went his way,
  And left the rock renowned,
And summer and winter his pilot star
  Hung bright o'er Plymouth Sound.

But it fell out, fell out at last,
  That he would put to sea,
To scan once more his lighthouse tower
  On the rock o' destiny.

And the winds broke, and the storm broke,
  And wrecks came plunging in ;
None in the town that night lay down
  Or sleep or rest to win.

The great mad waves were rolling graves,
  And each flung up its dead ;
The seething flow was white below,
  And black the sky o'erhead.

And when the dawn, the dull, gray dawn, —
  Broke on the trembling town,
And men looked south to the harbor mouth,
  The lighthouse tower was down.

Down in the deep where he doth sleep,
  Who made it shine afar,
And then in the night that drowned its light,
  Set, with his pilot star.

Many fair tombs in the glorious glooms
  At Westminster they show ;
The brave and the great lie there in state :
  Winstanley lieth low.

NOTES.

———◆———

PAGE 1.

THIS story I first wrote in prose, and it was published some years ago.

PAGE 100.

The name of the patriarch's wife is intended to be pronounced Nigh-loi-ya.

Of the three sons of Noah, — Shem, Ham, and Japhet, — I have called Japhet the youngest (because he is always named last), and have supposed that, in the genealogies where he is called "Japhet the elder," he may have received the epithet because by that time there were younger Japhets.

PAGE 167.

> The quivering butterflies in companies,
> That slowly crept adown the sandy marge,
> Like *living crocus beds.*

This beautiful comparison is taken from "The Naturalist on the River Amazons." "Vast numbers of orange-colored butterflies congregated on the moist sands. They assembled in densely-packed masses, sometimes two or three yards in circumference, their wings all held in an upright position, so that the sands looked as though variegated with *beds of crocuses.*"

14   S

"GLADYS AND HER ISLAND."

The woman is Imagination; she is brooding over what she brought forth.

The two purple peaks represent the domains of Poetry and of History.

The girl is Fancy.

"WINSTANLEY."

This ballad was intended to be one of a set, and was read to the children in the National Schools at Sherborne, Dorsetshire, in order to discover whether, if the actions of a hero were simply and plainly narrated, English children would like to learn the verses recording them, by heart, as their forefathers did.

Cambridge: Electrotyped and Printed by Welch, Bigelow, & Co.

MEMOIRS AND CORRESPONDENCE OF MADAME RECAMIER. Translated and Edited by MISS LUYSTER. One Volume, 12mo, with a finely engraved Portrait. Price, $2.00.

"The diversified contents of this volume can hardly fail to gain for it a wide perusal. It has the interest, in a greater or less degree, of history and romance; of truth stranger than fiction; of personal sketches; of the curious phases of an exceptional social life; of singular admixtures of piety and folly, of greatness and profligacy, fidelity and intrigue, all mingling or revealed in connection with the prolonged career of one who was, in certain respects, the most remarkable woman of her time." — *Boston Transcript.*

A PAINTER'S CAMP. Book I.: In England. Book II.: In Scotland. Book III.: In France. By PHILIP GILBERT HAMERTON. In one volume. 16mo. Pictorial title. Price, $1.50.

"In the pursuit of his profession as a landscape-painter, the author has not hesitated to plunge into the remote and unattractive nooks and corners of nature, gathering a rich store of materials for his pencil, and describing his whimsical experiences with a gayety and unction in perfect keeping with the subject. His account of the practical methods by which he conquered the difficulties of the position is instructive in the extreme, while the anecdotes and adventures which he relates with such exuberant fun make his book one of the most entertaining of the season." — *New York Tribune.*

CURIOUS MYTHS OF THE MIDDLE AGES. By S. BARING-GOULD. In one volume, 16mo. With Illustrations. Price, $1.50.

"A singular book, and a very interesting one to those who are fond of exploring the dark corners of literature and life, is 'Curious Myths of The Middle Ages,' by S. Baring-Gould, M. A. It treats of The Wandering Jew; Prester John; The Divining Rod; The Seven Sleepers of Ephesus; William Tell; The Dog Gellert; Tailed Men; Antichrist and Pope Joan; The Man in the Moon; The Mountain of Venus; Fatality of Numbers; The Terrestrial Paradise; bringing together many quaint and fanciful legends, exposing the fallacy of some popular beliefs, and suggesting topics for thought and investigation as to various psychological problems." — *Springfield Republican.*

SUNSHINE AND SHOWERS: Their Influences throughout Creation. A Compendium of Popular Meteorology. By ANDREW STEINMITZ, ESQ. The English Edition. One volume, post 8vo. With Illustrations. Price, $3.00.

"We have received from Roberts Brothers a delightful volume, published by Reeve & Co., London, entitled 'Sunshine and Showers: their Influences throughout Creation: by Andrew Steinmitz.' It is a compendium of popular meteorology. As a large portion of the conversation of human beings relates to the weather, we should judge that a book which enables one to talk intelligently about it would have an extensive circulation. It treats, in an intelligible way, of the arrangement of the atmosphere, the moisture in the air, the characteristics and meteorology of the seasons, the method of interpreting the barometer and the thermometer, the prediction of the weather and the explanation of popular weather prognostics, the curiosities of lightning, artificial rain, &c., and it answers the questions, 'What Becomes of the Sunshine?' and 'What Becomes of the Showers?' The science relating to all topics connected with the weather seems to have been mastered by the writer, and his volume is therefore full of surprising facts and ingenious theories." — *Boston Transcript.*

☞ *Mailed, post-paid, to any address, on receipt of the price, by the Publishers.*

CHRISTINA ROSSETTI'S POEMS. With Four Designs by D. G. ROSSETTI. One elegant 16mo volume. Price, $ 1.75.

"Two of the best of the younger poets of this generation are women — Jean Ingelow and Christina Rossetti. . . . The woman who could write the 'Songs of Seven,' and 'The High Tide on the Coast of Lincolnshire,' need not look to future successes for applause ; and there are many poems in this beautiful volume by Miss Rossetti which entitle her to a high place among the poets of the day." — *John G. Saxe.*

THE BOOK OF THE SONNET. By LEIGH HUNT and S. ADAMS LEE. A Posthumous Work by Hunt, *now first published from the original MSS.* In two beautiful post 8vo volumes. Price, $ 5.00.

"The genuine aroma of literature abounds in every page of Leigh Hunt's delicious Essay on the Sonnet. His mind shows itself imbued with a rich knowledge of his subject, and this, illumined by the evidence of a thorough and unaffected liking for it, makes him irresistible." — *London Saturday Review.*

ROBERT BUCHANAN'S POEMS. In one volume. 16mo. Cloth, gilt top. Price, $ 1.75.

"The volume is the work of a born poet. Let any one read the first and last poems in the collection, and he will not fail to read every line which intervenes between them. 'Langley Lane' is one of the tenderest, sweetest, most musical, and most original love-poems in the language." — *Boston Transcript.*

CHARLES LAMB. A Memoir. By BARRY CORNWALL. One volume, 16mo, with Profile Portrait of Lamb. Price, $ 1.75.

"We advise all young readers to approach Elia and Lamb's Life and Letters through this soft and exquisite prelude of Barry Cornwall's. . . . . Closing the book, and remembering that its writer is seventy-seven years old, and the sole survivor of those evenings which are as familiar to the lovers of Elia as if they had been themselves present, it lingers in the memory like a strain of the saddest and sweetest music." — *Harper's Monthly.*

THE GENIUS OF SOLITUDE. By REV. WM. R. ALGER, Author of "The Doctrine of a Future Life." One volume, 12mo. Price, $ 2.00.

"Mr. Alger's *Genius of Solitude* is the work of a scholar, of a man who has written critically and comprehensively on Oriental poetry, and on a branch of speculative psychology. It is, moreover, a book intended to have a practical effect — to teach men to dislike what is bad, and to admire and love what is good." — *London Chronicle.*

☞ *Mailed, post-paid, to any address, on receipt of the price, by the Publishers.*

www.ingramcontent.com/pod-product-compliance
Lightning Source LLC
Chambersburg PA
CBHW020844020726
47497CB00005B/1243